THE GEMINI RISING ROCKIN' MACHINE

WATCH THE PIG PEOPLE EATING DOG DAY APPLE PIE

Watch The Pig People Eating Dog Apple Pie
Featuring Books
Book Eleven: Dog Day Apple Pie
Book Twelve: The Pig People Are Back
Featuring The Lyrical Story And The Story
The Chemical Lightning Man

Copyright 2016 by The Gemini Rising Rockin' Machine
ISBN-13: 978-0692787991 (Gemini Rising Rockin' Machine, The)
ISBN-10: 0692787992

The characters and events described in this book are fictional. Any resemblance between the characters and any person including their names, living or dead, is purely coincidental.

Because of the mature themes presented within, reader discretion is advised.

For questions, comments you may send correspondence to.

thegeminirisingrockinmachine@twc.com

Official Website
www.thegeminirisingrockinmachine.com

Watch The Pig People Eating Dog Apple Pie (952.)

Oink-Oink – Bark-Bark
Watch-The-Pig-People
Eating-Dog-Apple-Pie
That's-Baked – With-Emptiness
That-Never – Fills-Them-Up

Oink-Oink – Bark-Bark
Watch-The-Pig-People
Eating-Dog-Apple-Pie
That's-High – On-Taxes
And-Gives-Them – The-Shits

(Chorus)
I Laugh – It's Useless – I'm Alone
While I Watch The Pig People
Eating Dog Apple Pie
That They Should Spit Back
Into The Faces Of The Dogs
For The People Are Not Pigs
No Matter What The Man Thinks

Oink-Oink – Bark-Bark
Watch-The-Pig-People
Eating-Dog-Apple-Pie
That's-Baked – With-Emptiness
That-Never – Fills-Them-Up

Oink-Oink – Bark-Bark
Watch-The-Pig-People
Eating-Dog-Apple-Pie
That's-High – On-Taxes
And-Gives-Them – The-Shits

(Chorus)
I Laugh – It's Useless – I'm Alone
While I Watch The Pig People
Eating Dog Apple Pie
That They Should Spit Back
Into The Faces Of The Dogs
For The People Are Not Pigs
No Matter What The Man Thinks

I Want Freedom (Not A Bunch Of Shit) (953.)

The-Dogs-Bark – The-Pigs-Oink
The-Predators-Smile – With-Freedom
As-The-Weak and The-Victims
Cry – Bleed and Die – Without-Justice

The-Dogs-Bark – The-Pigs-Oink
Spending-Millions – Being-Elected
While-The-Poor – Go-Hungry-Another-Day
The-Dogs-Bark – The-Pigs-Oink
Poisoned-Waters – Forest-Burning
While-Killers – Walk-The-Streets-Untouched

(Chorus)
I Want Freedom – Not A Bunch Of Shit
Do Me And The World A Favor
Keep Your Shit To Yourself
Because I Don't Want Or Need Shit
I Want Freedom – Not A Bunch Of Shit
I Also Prefer To Wipe My Ass
Before I Pull Up My Pants
In Case You're Wondering

I'd-Like to Throw – My-Shit at You
But-Why – Waste-My-Shit
Besides-You-Smell – Like-Shit-Already
And-I-Don't – Want to Feed-Your-Need
For-Your-Obsession to Shit-On-The-World

I'm-Rude – I'm-Obscene – I'm-Hateful
Well-No-Shit – Who-Taught-Me
To-Hate and Hardly-Wipe
So-I-Can-Be – Just-Like-You

(Chorus)
I Want Freedom – Not A Bunch Of Shit
Do Me And The World A Favor
Keep Your Shit To Yourself
Because I Don't Want Or Need Shit
I Want Freedom – Not A Bunch Of Shit
I Also Prefer To Wipe My Ass
Before I Pull Up My Pants
In Case You're Wondering

Book Eleven: Dog Day Apple Pie (Pages 4-33)

(Side One)
201. Dog Day Apple Pie (472.)
202. Brain Dead (873.)
203. For Everyone Song (288.)
204. Reach Reach (Free Food For The Poor) (604.)
   Everyday (But Not Today) **(879.)**
205. In The Morning (880.)

(Side Two)
206. Seeds Of Destruction (570.)
207. Dead Of Winter (Me, Myself & I Now) (215.)
208. Vote For Us (You Don't Matter) (487.)
209. Sex It Up (Too Many Taxes) (269.)
210. Nothing's Happening (167.)
   Why Was I The Way I Was **(878.)**

(Side Three)
211. Power (We Got The Power) (103.)
212. Power (We Took The Power) (104.)
(Love And Hate Duo)
   I. It's So Nice To Be Loved (361.)
213. **II.** It's So Nice To Be Hated (362.)
214. Kiss My Crap (887.)
215. Life Is A Fantasy (458.)

(Side Four)
216. Let's Get High (897.)
217. Fading Away (901)
(When There Are No Men On Earth Trilogy: 218-220)
218. This Is A Woman's World (793.)
219. Machine-Men (794.)
220. Sometimes You Don't Even Get What You Need (795.)
   I. Look In The Sky (We're Saved)
   II. Space-Men / Machine-Men
   III. You Will Learn To Love Us
      (Go Fly Back Into Outer Space)

(Bonus Songs)
Power Of The Rich (544.)
Fight, Fight (The Evil That Men Do) (593.)

201. Dog Day Apple Pie

Out of Thundering – Roars
Came-Silence and Darkness
Mankind-Left – On its Own
As-All-The-Power – Went-Out
Only the Sun is Our-Light

Panic – Rage – Violence
Flooding-Out – Into the Streets
The-Man – The-Law – Bring-Out
Their-Toys – Making-Ugly-Red
Mankind – Smears – Everywhere

(Chorus)
Dog Day Apple Pie – Chomp-Chomp-Chomp
Burning Inferno Of Cities – Blazing Out Of Control
Dog Day Apple Pie – Chomp-Chomp-Chomp
Hot Killing In The Streets – It's Everybody VS Everybody
Dog Day Apple Pie – Chomp-Chomp-Chomp – Eat It All Up

America-The-Beautiful – America-The-Great
Bleeding and Burning – With-No-Governments
All-The-Old – Have-Already-Fallen
The-Sick – The-Weak and The- Dying
Left-All-Alone – Without-Any-Help

(Chorus)
Dog Day Apple Pie – Chomp-Chomp-Chomp
Burning Inferno Of Cities – Blazing Out Of Control
Dog Day Apple Pie – Chomp-Chomp-Chomp
Hot Killing In The Streets – It's Everybody VS Everybody
Dog Day Apple Pie – Chomp-Chomp-Chomp – Eat It All Up

America – Thc-War-Ridden
America – The-Almost-Dead
Is-Crying-Out – In-Pain – As-Its-Citizens
Are-Being-Bought – Sold and Killed
Don't-Drop-Any – Of-That-Apple-Pie
We'll-Die-Of-Starvation – Its-All-We-Have-Left

(Repeat Chorus)

202. Brain Dead

Vote-Them-In – Vote-Them-Out
Different-Day – Same-Shit
Same as Four-Years – From-Now
Will-This-Endless – Cycle-Ever-End

Left-Right – Straight-Down the Middle
Your-Vote-Counts – Long as You – Follow-Them
Blindly – Questions-Are – For-The-Other-Side
Better be Careful – You're-Not – Being-Watched

(Chorus)
Brain Dead – Brain Dead
It's So Damn Contagious
Be The Same – Never Change
Brain Dead – Brain Dead
It's So Damn Contagious
Be The Same – Never Change

We're-All – Brain-Dead
When it Matters – The-Most
We-Know the Difference
It's-Just so Easy – Being-The-Same

Too-Bad-For-Us – Maybe-If-We-Stop
Believing – In-Heaven and Hell
Humanity-Will-Finally – Have a Chance
Then-Again – I-Doubt-It

(Chorus)
Brain Dead – Brain Dead
It's So Damn Contagious
Be The Same – Never Change
Brain Dead – Brain Dead
It's So Damn Contagious
Be The Same – Never Change

Is it Me – Is it The-World
Everything-Seems-Brain-Dead
I'm-Brain-Dead – Such a Shame
I'm-Brain-Dead – Such a Shame
Maybe-I-Could-Do-Something – Yeah-What
(Repeat Chorus)
6

203. For Everyone Song

I-Tried to Write a Song – For-Everyone
But-No-One – Liked-It at All
I-Decided to Keep it For-Myself
Using it For-Nothing at All
It-Stays in My-Mind – Like a Bad-Song
I-Can't-Help – Singing-Aloud
Making-Everyone – Like-Me-Even-Less

(Chorus)
Nobody Wants My
For Everyone Song
It's Too Different To Shine
Instead It Leaves A Bad Taste
That No One Can Spit Out

My-Song for Everyone – Keeps-Trying
To-Get-Itself – Out of My-Mind
Still-Believing – That it Can-Help
Bring-Peace and Love to The-World
I-Keep-On – Trying to Tell-It
That it Doesn't – Stand a Chance
There is Too-Much-War and Mankind
Still-Craves-Blood – Way-Too-Much

(Chorus)
Nobody Wants My
For Everyone Song
It's Too Different To Shine
Instead It Leaves A Bad Taste
That No One Can Spit Out

My-Mind's-Gone-On – Trying to Forget
Helping-My-Song for Everyone – Lose-Strength
It's-Now-Only a Bit-Piece – That
Comes to My-Mind – Once in Awhile
I-Can't-Wait – 'Til it's Dead and Gone
What a Mistake it Truly-Was
Hopefully-In a Little-While – Everyone-Will
Forget-About – My for Everyone-Song
And-Start – Liking-Me-Again

(Repeat Chorus)

204. Reach Reach (Free Food For The Poor)

I-Don't – Mind the Pain
It-Keeps – Me-Strong
Life is Marvelous – But
Living-It – Is so Scarring

Hellish-Wars and Starvation
Roams-Hungrily – Across-Our-Globe
It's-Killing-Us to Our-Graves
We-Must-Demand – Everyday
Having a Life – Worth-Living

(Chorus)
Reach Reach – No More Lies
Reach Reach – No More Pain
Reach Reach – Free Food For The Poor
Reach Reach – No More War
Reach Reach – No More Death
Reach Reach – Free Food For The Poor
Reach Reach – In Deep You Uncaring
Reach Reach – Free Food For The Poor

Take-Away-The-Tight – Bloody-Closed-Fist
Bring-Forth – Spoonfuls of Love
Tranquility is a Beautiful-Thing – Hate
Blood-Slaughter is Not-Very-Nice

We-Don't – Want-Everything
We-Just-Want-Enough to Live-Great
With-More of The-Means – Around
For-Us to Be-Allowed to Make it With
That's-Not-Asking too Much – Is-It

(Chorus)
Reach Reach – No More Lies
Reach Reach – No More Pain
Reach Reach – Free Food For The Poor
Reach Reach – No More War
Reach Reach – No More Death
Reach Reach – Free Food For The Poor
Reach Reach – In Deep You Uncaring
Reach Reach – Free Food For The Poor

Everyday (But Not Today)

Down and Out – Just-Don't-Care
What is The-Answer – I'll-Never-Know
Summer's-Wind – Heats-My-Face
While-Walking-Among-Them to My-Day

Sad-Eyes – Filled-With-Despair
Evil-Eyes – Filled-With-Hate
Look-Through-Me – Seeing-No-One
Until-The-Day – I-Get in Their-Way
It's-Not-Their-Fault – It's the World's

(Chorus)
Everyday Is The Same
Everyday I Just Go On And On
Everyday – But Not Today
No-More – Not Today
Life Is For Living To Its Fullest
Not Living Everyday The Same Way
Until The Day – Fate Decides
To Take My Life Away

Blood-Stains – That-Wall
Look-Across the Street
Blood-Stains – That-Wall as Well
Mister-Death – Never-Gets a Coffee-Break

Freedom is For-Sale
While-I'm - Always-Broke
Life is Just – One-Long-Thread
That-Keeps on Being-Pulled-On
'Til-The-Day it Unravels and Flies-Away

(Chorus)
Everyday Is The Same
Everyday I Just Go On And On
Everyday – But Not Today
No-More – Not Today
Life Is For Living To Its Fullest
Not Living Everyday The Same Way
Until The Day – Fate Decides
To Take My Life Away

205. In The Morning

Let's go Baby – Time to Get-Going
Everyone – Yes-Everyone
Is-Going to Be – Partying-Tonight
We-Have to Arrive at The-Perfect-Time

Let-Me-Look at You – Baby
You-Look so Fine and Sweet
Let-Me-Touch and Kiss-You
Then-We're-Gone

(Chorus)
In The Morning
Everything Will Seem Better
In The Morning
I Will Wake Up And Stretch
In The Morning – I'll-Do
My Very Best To Lie To Myself
That Tonight Never Happen

Driving-Down – The-High-Road of Life
Everything's-Fine – Pull-Over
Time to Show – Our-Fans – Our-Faces
Life is Great – You-First-Baby – Enjoy-It

Bang – Bang – Two-Shots-Fired
I-Watch in Silence and Fear
As-The-Love of My-Life – Dies
While-She's – Closing the Door

(Chorus)
In The Morning
Everything Will Seem Better
In The Morning
I Will Wake Up And Stretch
In The Morning – I'll-Do
My Very Best To Lie To Myself
That Tonight Never Happen

206. Seeds Of Destruction

Mankind-Walked-Out of Their-Caves
Searching for Fire a New-Way of Life
Gathering and Taking-Away
They-Moved-On and On
Leaving – They'd-Been-There
For the Animals to Know and Fear

(Chorus)
Mankind The Smartest
Mankind The Weakest
Made The World Their Own
As They Planted Their
Seeds Of Destruction

Buildings-That-Reach – The-Sky
Mother-Earth is Covered
With-Tons of Steel and Glass
Blocking-Out – All of The-Sun
The-Rich – Get-Driven-Home
Far-Away – From-Their-Cities
While the Poor – Hold-Their-Breaths
Hoping-They-Survive – Another-Night

(Chorus)
Mankind The Smartest
Mankind The Weakest
Made The World Their Own
As They Planted Their
Seeds Of Destruction

Star-Ships in The-Galaxy
Mother-Earth is Long-Dead
The-Rich-Flew-Away – With-Force
As-The-Poor – Died-Without-Hope
Earth-Number-Two is Colonized
She-Is-Very-Very – Different
Aliens-Land and Get-Mad to What-Mankind
Did to Their-Planet – Ray-Guns – Pulled-Out
Fired-Everywhere – Mankind-Exists – No-More

(Repeat Chorus)

207. Dead Of Winter (Me, Myself & I Now)

I'm-Still-Living – In-The-Streets
Mr. – Me-Myself & I – Himself
Time-Has-Taken – Its-Toll
I'm-Way too Old – Now
To be Living – Like-This-Anymore

Summer-Time is Hellish-Hot
Sidewalk-Will – Burn-Your-Flesh
While-The-Streets – Eat-Your-Soul
Winter-Is a Long-Lasting
Freezing-Cold – Ruthless-Beast
That-Makes-You-Feel – Like it Can
Make-You-Die – Unless-You're-Lucky

(Chorus)
The Cold That Rushes – Through The City
In The Dead Of Winter – Is So Intensely Freezing
My Old Bones Feel Like – They're Going To Break
Will Someone Please Help – Me, Myself & I Now
Don't Wanna Die – Stuck To The Frozen Winter's Ground

Below-Zero – The-Wind-Roars
Bringing-Wave – After-Wave of
Flying-Snow-Drifts – That-Cover-Everything
I'm so Cold – I-Can't-Stop-Moving
Gotta-Keep-Going-On or I-Will-Die
In-This-Winter's – Bitter-Night

Lose-Track of Time – I-Have to Smile
Fooling-Myself – Tonight is The-Night
The-Very-Last-One of My-Life
This-Winter's-Beast is Hungry
Gobbling-Up – The-Street-Souls
Mine is One-More to Help – Fill-Its-Belly-Up

(Chorus)
The Cold That Rushes – Through The City
In The Dead Of Winter – Is So Intensely Freezing
My Old Bones Feel Like – They're Going To Break
Will Someone Please Help – Me, Myself & I Now
Don't Wanna Die – Stuck To The Frozen Winter's Ground

208. Vote For Us (You Don't Matter)

Can-They – Feed-The-Poor
Damn-Right – They-Can
Will – They
Not-Today – They-Won't

Food-Costs – Too-Much
The-Poor – Can't-Afford
So-They – Hold it Over
All-The-Poor-Heads
Like-They're – Giving-Them-Something

(Chorus)
Vote For Us
You Don't Matter
Just Do It Already
And Shut The Hell Up
For We Got More
Important Things To Do
Than Spend Time – Wasting It On You

We-Have to Rule – The-Country
Controlling – Americans
All-At a Time – Is-The-Way
They're so Lost and Scared
And-We-Have – All-The-Answers

Filled-With – Friendly-Lies
That-We – Proudly-Tell-Them
As-We-Wave – Our-Goodbyes
Wanting to Hold – Our-Noses
Because-You-Poor – Smell so Bad

(Chorus)
Vote For Us
You Don't Matter
Just Do It Already
And Shut The Hell Up
For We Got More
Important Things To Do – Than
Spend Time – Wasting It On You

13

209. Sex It Up (Too Many Taxes)

Tax-Our-Food – Tax-Our-Water
Tax-Our-Fun – Tax-Our-Lives
Even – Tax-Us to Death

Wouldn't-Be so Bad if Our-Taxes
Did-Some-Good – What-We-Pay-In
Should be More – Than-Enough to Feed
All-The-Poor – Get-Them – Off-The-Streets
Into-Warm-Homes – Filled-With-Love
But-This-Never-Happens so I-Say

(Chorus #1)
Go Ahead Everybody – Sex It Up
This Is About The Only Thing
That We Don't Have To Pay Taxes On Yet
Go Ahead Everybody – Sex It Up
Show Them That We Can Screw Too

(Chorus #2)
Go Ahead Everybody – Sex It Up
What Could You Possibly Be Doing
That Is Less Taxing On You Than Sex
Go Ahead Everybody – Sex It Up
Before The Man Taxes Our Sex To Boredom

Not-Everyone – Can-Make-It-Great
Most of Us – Just-Live – Day to Day
Doing-Without – Wishing and Dreaming
That-Our-Lives – Can-Rise-Up
From-Out Of All-Your – Taxing-Heels

Tax-Me – Tax-We – Tax-Us-All
What-Can-We-Do – But-Pay-You
Knowing-That – You're-Going-To
Blow-It-All – On a Bunch of Nothing
That is Not – Helping-Anyone-Out
Except of Course – All of You

(Repeat Chorus #1)
(Repeat Chorus #2)

I-Don't-Know – About-The-Rest of You
I and The-Other-I's – I-Know
Feel-Like – We're-All-Being-Used
And-Not-Even – Thanked-For-It
Not-Even-Given a Coffee – Or a Cookie

So-I-Say – Hell-With-It – Let's-Have-Some-Fun
1-2-3 – Let's-Sex it Up – Everyone
Real-Good and For a Really – Long-Time
Because-There-Are – Too-Many-Taxes – And-We
Might as Well – Get-All-The-Screwing – Out of Us
While-We're-Being – Screwed-Out of All-Our-Money

(Chorus #1)
Go Ahead Everybody – Sex It Up
This Is About The Only Thing
That We Don't Have To Pay Taxes On Yet
Go Ahead Everybody – Sex It Up
Show Them That We Can Screw Too

(Chorus #2)
Go Ahead Everybody – Sex It Up
What Could You Possibly Be Doing
That Is Less Taxing On You Than Sex
Go Ahead Everybody – Sex It Up
Before The Man Taxes Our Sex To Boredom

(The Man Speaks To We The People)
Stop-It – Stop-It-Now – Sex-Having-People
This is All – You-Do-Now – You-Don't-Even-Work
Do-You-Think – It's a Democracy of Sex-Having
You-Have-Pushed and Thrust-Way-Too-Much
Since-This is Your-Favorite – It's to Be-Taxed-Thickly
All-Together-Everyone – Sing-Along to Our-New-Tax-Song

Pay-Pay-Pay – Your-Sex-Tax
Pay-Pay-Pay – For-Your-Sexual-Ways
Pay-Pay-Pay – Or-We'll-Take-Away
What-You-Have-Sex-With – Oh-Yes-We-Will
You-Can-Bet – Your-Sex-Tax-On-That

(Repeat Chorus #1)
(Repeat Chorus #2)

15

210. Nothing's Happening

Life-Is a Hard – Ass-Funk
Coming-Down on Us
Making it Seem – Unbearable
Making it Hard to Breathe
With-All-The-Hate – Breeding-With
Violence and Bloodshed – All-Around

Making it Easy to Say – Hell-With-It
Staying-With – Who-We-Love
Not-Getting-Out-There and Sharing
With-Someone-Else – What-We-Have
Letting-Them-Know – The-Best-Thing
In-The-Whole-Wide-World – Is-Love

(Chorus)
Nothing's Happening
With Love – That's A Shame
Seems All The Earth's Children
Want To Hate Instead – Making
Nothing Happen But The Same

Some-May-Say – It-Does-Some-Good
It's-Better-Than – Nothing at All
But-The-Spreading of Empty-Love
Does so Much-Damage
It's a Form of Evil-Itself
No Matter-What – The-Sayers-Say

In-Truth it Has a Short – Shelf-Life
It-Consists of Nothing but Emptiness
Which-Dies-Before – It-Gets a Chance to Grow
Leaving-Hardened-Emotions – In-All of Us
Making-Walls – Appear-Everywhere – For
No-One-Around to Care to Break-Through

(Chorus)
Nothing's Happening
With Love – That's A Shame
Seems All The Earth's Children
Want To Hate Instead – Making
Nothing Happen But The Same

16

Why Was I The Way I Was

I'm-The-Cold – Chill of Reality
That-Never – Escapes-Your-Mind
Look at The-Window-Pane
Does it Make – You-Feel-Safe
When-The-Sun – Shines-Though-It

Life-Was at Its-Best – Years-Ago
As-You-Wipe – Dust-From-Your-Eyes
Listen to The-Distance – Hear a Whisper
Your-Life-Calling-Out – For-Its-Ending
Listen to The-Sadness of An-Uninspired

(Chorus)
Why Was I The Way I Was
Life Could Have Been So Grand
Why Was I The Way I Was
It's Too Late To Start Over
Why Was I The Way I Was
I Live A Life Full Of Regrets
Each And Every Unfilled Day

The-Road-Not-Taken is The-First
The-Last-Nail – In-Your-Coffin
You-Have – The-World to Blame
Even-Though – You-Know-It's a Lie
You've-Never – Told-Even-Once

Life-Was at Its-Best – Years-Ago
As-You-Wipe – Dust-From-Your-Eyes
Listen to The-Distance – Hear a Whisper
Your-Life-Calling-Out – For-Its-Ending
Listen to The-Sadness of An-Uninspired

(Chorus)
Why Was I The Way I Was
Life Could Have Been So Grand
Why Was I The Way I Was
It's Too Late To Start Over
Why Was I The Way I Was
I Live A Life Full Of Regrets
Each And Every Unfilled Day

211. Power (We Got The Power)

We're-The-Man – Worship or Else
Doesn't-Matter – Who-You-Are – You-Will-Follow
Our-Rules – Wanting to Worship-Us
We-The-Right to Mold – This-Country
Into-What – We-The-Man – Your
Marvelous-Government – Wants-It to Be

We're-The-Man – What-Can-You-Do
That's-Right – Nothing-And
Follow-In-Line – Everybody-Has to
Be-The-Same – Poor and Needing
With-Your-Hands-Out – So-We-Can
Give-You-What – We-Think-You-Need

(Chorus)
Power – We Got The Power
To Keep You Down
If You Don't Comply
We Got Enough Power
To Government – You Down
Power – We Got The Power

We're-The-Man – There's so Many of You
We're-Just a Few – You-Should-Feel-Lucky
That-We-Still – Allow-You the Right to Vote
You-Riot – Like a Bunch of Ingrates – We're-Not
Protecting-Your-Rights – Who-Do-You – Think-You-Are
Our-Needs – Wants – Always-Come-First

Great-Thing-About-This – You-Will-Forget
About it Real-Fast – When-We-Start-Up
Something-Special – Be-Behind-Us as We-Get
This-Country – Out of Its-Next – Great-Big-Calamity

(Chorus)
Power – We Got The Power
To Keep You Down
If You Don't Comply
We Got Enough Power
To Government – You Down
Power – We Got The Power

18

212. Power (We Took The Power)

True-Freedom – Even-Though it's Here
Feels-Strange – Almost-Unreal
Can-This be True – Gonna-Take-My-Chances
Walk-My-City's-Streets at This-Midnight-Hour

City's-Filled-Up – Tonight
People-Everywhere – Talking to Each-Other
No-Fighting – No-Yelling of Rage
Looking-Around – I'm-Surrounded by Different
For-The-First-Time – I-Don't-Feel-Scared
Seems-Being-Different is Not-Important-Anymore

(Chorus)
Power – We Took The Power
The Man Was A Bunch Of Takers
Doing Whatever They Wanted
By Voting Them Out
We Brought Forth – A New Beginning
Power – We Took The Power

The-First-Night – Led to The-Next-Night
This-Was a Fresh-Start – For-All of Us
It-Was-Intense and Overwhelming
There-Were a Few – That-Could-Not-Change
Got-Their-Shoes – Stepped-On – Brought
Yesterday-Back-Up – With-All-Its-Rage

Rest of Us – Held on Tighter – Together
Knowing-What – We-Had to Do
Showing-Them-The-Way to Enlightenment
That it's No-Longer – Right to Hate
Because of Race or Gender – That-They
Can-Forget-About – Religious-Difference – Since
We-Now-All-Belong to The-Church of No-God

(Chorus)
Power – We Took The Power
The Man Was A Bunch Of Takers
Doing Whatever They Wanted
By Voting Them Out
We Brought Forth – A New Beginning
Power – We Took The Power

19

I. It's So Nice To Be Loved (Re-Print)

It's so Very-Sad to Me – That-Everybody-Now-Seems
Not to Want-Love – They're so Down – Into-Their-Lives

It's-Just – Speeding-Away so Fast
When-They-Finally-Have – The-Time to Slow-Down
There's-No-One-Around – For-Them to Love

(Chorus)
It's So Nice To Be Loved
I Tell Ya
It's So Nice To Be Loved
You Know It
It's So Nice To Be Loved
Come On Everybody
It's So Nice To Be Loved

I-Don't-Have the Best-Life – A-Lot of Times
It's-One-Big-Old-Bummer – But-I-Never-Let-Life
Bring-Me-Down – Too-Far – Because – I-Have a Lot of Love
Inside-My-Heart – To-Keep-Me-Going-On

So-When-Life – Starts-To – Bring-Me-Down
I-Grab a Hold of My-Love – And-Give-Her a Great-Big-Kiss

(Chorus)
It's So Nice To Be Loved
I Tell Ya
It's So Nice To Be Loved
You Know It
It's So Nice To Be Loved
Come On Everybody
It's So Nice To Be Loved

If-You-Ever – Want to Know – How-Great-Love-Can-Be
Give-Me a Call – I'll-Let-You-Know

'Til-Then – Try-To – Do-Your-Best
To-Bring-Some-Love – Into-Your-Heart
Your-Life-Will-Be – So-Much-Better
Falling – And-Being – In-Love

(Repeat Chorus)
20

213. II. It's So Nice To Be Hated

It's so Very-Sad to Me – That-Everybody-Now-Seems
Not to Want-Hate– They're so Up – Into-Their-Lives

It's-Just – Speeding-Away so Fast
When-They-Finally-Have – The-Time to Slow-Down
There's-No-One-Around – For-Them to Hate

(Chorus)
It's So Nice To Be Hated
I Tell Ya
It's So Nice To Be Hated
You Know It
It's So Nice To Be Hated
Come On Everybody
It's So Nice To Be Hated

I-Don't-Have the Best-Life – A-Lot of Times
It's-One-Big-Old-Bummer – But-I-Never-Let-Life
Bring-Me-Down – Too-Far – Because – I-Have a Lot of Hate
Inside-My-Heart – To-Keep-Me-Going-On

So-When-Life – Starts-To – Bring-Me-Down-Up
I-Grab a Hold of My-Un-Love – And-Give-Her a Great-Big-Bite

(Chorus)
It's So Nice To Be Hated
I Tell Ya
It's So Nice To Be Hated
You Know It
It's So Nice To Be Hated
Come On Everybody
It's So Nice To Be Hated

If-You-Ever – Want to Know – How-Great-Hate-Can-Be
Give-Me a Call – I'll-Let-You-Know

'Til-Then – Try-To – Do-Your-Best
To-Bring-Some-Hate – Into-Your-Heart
Your-Life-Will-Be – So-Much-Better
Not-Falling and Being-In-Love

(Chorus)

214. Kiss My Crap

Watch-Me-Walk
Listen to Me-Talk
Give-Me – That-Look
Like-I – Don't-Belong

I'm-Not-Fresh – I'm a Dirty-Soul
Tarnished – From-The-Streets
Streets-That-Bleed – Streets-That-Die
Yet – I – Survive

(Chorus)
Tell You What Man
Kiss My Crap
I Don't Need Your Nod
Kiss My Crap
I'm Doing Just Fine
Tell You What Man
Take My Crap Home And Eat It Up

Shake-With-Fear – You're a Man
Pull-Your-Gun – I-Have-No-Knife
Standing-Still – I-Never-Show-Fear
Blink-Your-Eyes is All-I-Need

Wanting-Out of This is All-You-Want
Shake-With-Fear – You're a Man
Pull-Your-Trigger or Walk-Away
I-Have a Lover – That-Needs-Loving

(Chorus)
Tell You What Man
Kiss My Crap
I Don't Need Your Nod
Kiss My Crap
I'm Doing Just Fine
Tell You What Man
Take My Crap Home And Eat It Up

215. Life Is A Fantasy

Can-You-See – That-Touch
Can-You-Smell – That-Sound
Do-You-Know – What-You're-Doing
You're-Flying-High – In-Your-Mind
With-Your-Feet – Still-Planted
On the Ground – Like a Statue

All in Your-Mind – You-Live
Climbing to The-Top – You-Go
What is That – Heavy-Ticking
It's-Your-Heart – Racing-Faster
Matching-Your-Mind's – Speeding

(Chorus)
Life Is A Fantasy – In Your Mind
Is True Reality – Biting At Your Brain
Life Is A Fantasy – In Your Mind
Have Some Fun Mind Surfing
Then Wake Up Miserable To Life
Life Is A Fantasy – Only In Your Mind

You're-In-It so Thick
You-Become – All by Yourself
That-You-Stink to Low-Hell
Your-Body is Like an Awkward
Piece of Unneeded – Human-Machinery

You're-Fading-Away as I
Try to Shake – You-Awake
Your-Fantasy – Took a Last-Turn
As-You-Made – Yourself-Fall
Your-Mind – Your-Last-Morsel of Life
Mind-Surfed – To a Lost-Paradise
You and It-Clicked – Then-Faded-Away

(Chorus)
Life Is A Fantasy – In Your Mind
Is True Reality – Biting At Your Brain
Life Is A Fantasy – In Your Mind
Have Some Fun Mind Surfing
Then Wake Up Miserable To Life
Life Is A Fantasy – Only In Your Mind

216. Let's Get High

Look at The-Bloodstains
Will-They – Dry-Away
Pass-Me – That-Joint
Let's-Walk – Let's-Get-High

Look at Those – Dead-Bodies
Wonder-How-Long – They-Been-There
Pass-Me – That-Joint
Let's-Run – Let's-Get-High

(Chorus)
Let's Get High – Let's Get High
Let's Get High – While
Bombs Of Death
Pummel The Earth
Let's Get High – Let's Get High
Let's Get High – While
World War III Starts And Finishes
Let's Get High – Let's Get High
Let's Get High – Before We Die

Look-Up – Into-The-Blue-Sky
Atomic-Bombs – Are-Heading-Our-Way
Pass-Me – That-Joint
Let's-Sit on The-Ground – Let's-Get-High

Look at That – Wave of Death
Coming-Our-Way
Pass-Me – That-Joint
I-Want – One-More-Toke

(Chorus)
Let's Get High – Let's Get High
Let's Get High – While
Bombs Of Death
Pummel The Earth
Let's Get High – Let's Get High
Let's Get High – While
World War III Starts And Finishes
Let's Get High – Let's Get High
Let's Get High – Before We All Die

217. Fading Away

Live-Bad – Live-Great
In-The-End
It-Does-Not-Matter

Time is Time
Everyone-Has – Their-Amount
When it's Gone – You're-Dead

(Chorus)
I'm Fading Away
My Time Is Over
I'm Fading Away
Soon – I Will Die
I'm Fading Away
Later – I Will Feed The Clay
I'm Fading Away
Nothing I Can Do About It

Mr.-Death – How-Do-You-Do
I'm a Man – With-One-Breath-Left
Count to Ten – Take-Me-Away

Hello-God – How-Do-You-Do
I'm a Soul – That-Use to Be a Man
I'm-Ready for My-Judgment

Hello-Satan – How-Do-You-Do
I'm a Sad – Damned-Soul
That's-Not-Good-Enough for Heaven
Be-Gentle

(Chorus)
I'm Fading Away
My Time Is Over
I'm Fading Away
Soon – I Will Die
I'm Fading Away
Later – I Will Feed The Clay
I'm Fading Away
Nothing I Can Do About It

(When There Are No Men On Earth Trilogy: 218-220)

218. This Is A Woman's World

(The Earth Women Sing)

Mankind – Our-Oppressors
We-Are-Woman – Hear-Us-Moan
Your-Dirty – Loving-Dolls
That-You-Need and Love so Much
We-Are-Woman – What-Can-We-Do
Out of Nowhere – Sickness
Man-The-Strong – Man-The-Dying
We-Are-Woman – We-Are-Pure
We-Are-Woman – We-Live-Forever

(Chorus)
This Is A Woman's World
With No Man Around Alive
To Bring Us Flowers And Jewelry
This Is A Woman's World
Metal Is Close Enough To Flesh
Who Cares – They're Just Tools
This Is A Woman's World
Ladies Get Use To Change

Man is Hard to Create
Their-Heart so Easy
Their-Peckers – Are-Another-Thing
We-Are-Woman – What-Can-We-Do
Stupid – Dumb – Men
Why-Did-All of You – Have to Die
Flesh is Better – Than-Metal
We-Miss-Your – Touch so Much

(Chorus)
This Is A Woman's World
With No Man Around Alive
To Bring Us Flowers And Jewelry
This Is A Woman's World
Metal Is Close Enough To Flesh
Who Cares – They're Just Tools
This Is A Woman's World
Ladies Get Use To Change
26

219. Machine-Men

(The Earth Women Sing)

Machine-Men – With-Skins of Clay
Insides of Wires – With-No-Personality
Were-Created to Serve-Woman
They-Served – Their-Purpose – but

We-Got-Bored – With-Them
Gave-Them – The-Abilities to
Turn-Them-On – Make-Them-Laugh
Make-Them-Feel-Love and Jealousy

(Chorus)
Machine Men Have Taken Over
Once A Tool – Now The Superior
They Pay No Attention To Woman's Needs
All Machine Men Do Now Is Have Sex
Like They Were Programmed To Do
Only Now They Want To – Because
Machine Men Are Very, Very Horny

We-Women – Feel so Used
Machine-Men – Never-Get-Sick
Machine-Men – Never-Have to Sleep
Machine-Men – Never-Allow-Us to Say-No

Lord-Help-Us – Lord-Save-Us
Give-Our-Machine-Men – Humanity
Give-Our-Machine-Men – Souls
Lord-Help-Us – Lord-Save-Us
Cast-Our-Machine-Men – Off-This-World
Give-Us-Women – Another-Choice

(Chorus)
Machine Men Have Taken Over
Once A Tool – Now The Superior
They Pay No Attention To Woman's Needs
All Machine Men Do Now Is Have Sex
Like They Were Programmed To Do
Only Now They Want To – Because
Machine Men Are Very, Very Horny

220. Sometimes You Don't Even Get What You Need (In 3 Parts)

I. Look In The Sky (We're Saved)

(The Earth Women Sing)

What-Have-We-Done – Why oh Why
Could-We-Not be Happy – All-Alone
We-Are-Woman – We-Are-Filled-With-Love
Some-Didn't-Mind – Some-Missed-Man
We-Are-Woman – Hear-Us-Moan-No-More
For-The-Lust of Man – That-We-Created

Fake-Men – Made-Out of Metal
We-Lost-Control – We-Lost-Everything
Everyday-More-Sex – With-No-Humanity
Everyday-Machine-Men – Lust-Us to Death
Why-Can't-We-Women – Get-What-We-Want

(Chorus)
Can It Be True – We're Saved
Look In The Sky – We're Saved
Space-Men From Space – Have Arrived
Space-Men Oh Space-Men – Help Us
Destroy Our Metal-Men Oppressors
Then Space-Men You Can Have Us

(The Machine Men Sing)

We-Metal-Men – Look-Into-The-Sky
Space-Men are Coming to Take-Our-Women
First-Blood – Doesn't-Count – Eventually
Space-Men – Will-Have to Land
We-Metal-Men – We-Will be In-Waiting – We'll-Save
Our-Human-Women – From-The-Evil-Space-Men

(Chorus)
Can It Be True – We're Saved
Look In The Sky – We're Saved
Space-Men From Space – Have Arrived
Space-Men Oh Space-Men – Help Us
Destroy Our Metal-Men Oppressors
Then Space-Men You Can Have Us

II. Space-Men / Machine-Men

(The Earth Women Sing)
We're-Saved – We're-Saved
Space-Ships – Shooting-Laser-Beams
Destroying-Many – Machine-Men
Finally-We-Women – Will-Be-Free
No-More-Oppressors – Oppressing-Us

(Chorus)
War On Earth – War For The Earth Woman
Space-Men VS Machine-Men
Who Will Win The War
Who Will Own Earth's Women

(The Machine Men Sing)
We-Are-Pure – We-Are-Machine-Men
Space-Ships – Shooting-Laser-Beams
Flesh-Bag-Cowards – Land-We-Dare-You
Got to Hide – Have to Wait – We-Will-Win
No-Space-Men – Will-Have-Our-Women
They-Created-Us to Worship-Us

(Chorus)
War On Earth – War On Earth
Space-Men VS Machine-Men
Who Will Win The War
Who Will Own Earth's Women

(The Space Men Sing)
What-The-Hell is Going-On
Machine-Men – With-Our-Women
How-Did-This-Happen – Does-Not-Matter
We-Removed – Their-Ugly-Male-Counterparts
We-Will-Remove – Their-Ugly-Machine-Men
All-Our-Women-Are-Dead – Big-Mistake
Earth-Women – Will-Now be Our-Brides

(Chorus)
War On Earth – War On Earth
Space-Men VS Machine-Men
Who Will Win The War
Who Will Own Earth's Women

III. You Will Learn To Love Us (Go Fly Back Into Outer Space)

(The Space Men Sing)
So-Many of Us – Have-Died
All-In the Pursuit of Woman
We-Have-None – Earth-Women-Are-Fine
No- Fuss – No-Muss = Disaster

Were-These-Earth-Women – Worth-All-The-Loss
Will-They-Conform to Our-Way – To-Our-God
They-Look so Simple – They-Are-Weird-Shaped
They-Are-Better – Than-No-Woman at All
All-Right-Men – The-Time-Is at Hand – Ready
Go-Round-Up – Your-New-Alien-Bride to Be

(Chorus)
S-M: You Will Learn To Love Us
You Will Show Us Respect
You Are Ours To Own – Forever
E-W: Space-Men Bastards From Space
Go Fly Back Into Outer Space
We Don't Want Any Of Your Alien Love

(The Earth Women Sing)
We-Women – Are-The-Rose
Males-In-All-Their-Forms – Are-The-Thorn
Can't-We-Ever – Get a Fair-Shake
First-Came-Mankind – Second-Came-Machine-Men
Now-Third – Space-Men – With-Weird-Ugly-Bodies

This is not Fair – We-Deserve-Better-Than-Living
On a Alien-World – Being-Brides to Alien-Husbands
We-Are-Woman – We-Will-Survive – We-Will
Make-Them-Pay – Will-Bitch-Their-Ears-Off – Stupid
Space-Men-Don't-Realize – What-They've-Gotten-Into

(Chorus)
S-M: You Will Learn To Love Us
You Will Show Us Respect
You Are Ours To Own – Forever
E-W: Space-Men Bastards From Space
Go Fly Back Into Outer Space
We Don't Want Any Of Your Alien Love

Power Of The Rich (544.) (Bonus Song)

The-Poor-Are-Poor – Don't-You-Get-That
They-Don't-Have – Enough to Eat
They-Sleep on The-Ground
Don't-Matter to Rich-People
That-Spend – More on Dry-Cleaning
Than-The-Poor – With-Houses
Spend on Not-Enough – Dinner to Eat

(Chorus)
Power Of The Rich
With Big Bags Of Green
Waiting On Us To Take Away
This Is What This Country Needs
Power Of The Rich
With Big Bags Of Green
Makes This Country – Quite Obscene

Rich-Don't-Care – Because-The-Poor
Don't-Spend-Money – Give-Them-Some
It-Must be Nice – Not-Having to Worry
Doctors – Lawyers – All in Waiting
For-You – When-You-Need-Them
Get-This – Most of The-Really-Poor
Don't-Even-Have a Bathroom to Use

(Chorus)
Power Of The Rich
With Big Bags Of Green
Waiting On Us To Take Away
This Is What This Country Needs
Power Of The Rich
With Big Bags Of Green
Makes This Country – Quite Obscene

The-Government – Loves-The-Poor
That's-Why-They-Make so Many of Them
They-Give-The-Poor – Healthcare
While-Smacking – Their-Hands-Away
If-The-Government – Really-Cared
They-Would – Cut-All-The-Cost
That-The-Poor – Have to Pay
(Repeat Chorus)
31

Fight, Fight (The Evil That Men Do) (593.) (Bonus Song)

I-Speak for Myself – I-Think for Myself
I-Don't-Fear-Death – I-Live-Everyday
I-Can-Only – Die-Once

When-I-Wake-Every-Day – I-Want-Peace
The-World-Does-Not – Let-There be War
Don't-Blame-We – We-Only-Want-Peace

My-Hands-Are-Broken – My-Heart is Scarred
I-Almost-Died – The-Evil-That-Men-Do
Never-Yield – Never-Stop

(Chorus)
Fight, Fight – The Evil That Men Do
Fight, Fight – 'Til All Evil Is Gone
Fight, Fight – The Evil That Men Do
Fight, Fight – 'Til Earth Bleeds No More

I'm-Down and Bleeding – Never-Will-I
Kneel and Join-Evil
I-Have-No-God – Only-One-Answer
Make-Them-Feel – Like-Fools for Believing

Reach-Out – Take-My-Hand
Hand-Over-Hand-Over-Hand
Will-Be – Our-Strength
I'll-Disappear – Without-You
Do-Nothing – Let-The-Same – Stay-Around
It's-Up to You – I-Understand
Why-Should-You
What's-The-Harm – In-Heaven

Because-Heaven – Was-Created
By a Ruler – That-No-Longer-Wanted
The-Poor to Have a Choice

(Chorus)
Fight, Fight – The Evil That Men Do
Fight, Fight – 'Til All Evil Is Gone
Fight, Fight – The Evil That Men Do
Fight, Fight – 'Til Earth Bleeds No More

YOUR OWN MIND ROCKIN' PAGE #1

Book Twelve: The Pig People Are Back (Pages 34-65)

(Side One)
221. The Pig People Are Back (441.)
222. Make Love Not War (663.)
223. My Wish Is (312.)
224. What's Next (791.)
225. Save The World (947.)
    I. Wood And Metal Eaters
    II. Flesh And Bone Eaters

(Side Two)
226. Kick You In The Mind (574.)
227. Prick Of Flesh (520.)
228. The Blue Planet Red And Dead (511.)
229. It Was Just Yesterday (119.)
    Life Is Too Short **(912.)**
230. My Force (399.)

(Side Three)
231. Time Is In My Eyes / Weak God People (668.)
232. Freedom With Sex (669.)
233. Tag,Tag (Tag You're It) (670.)
234. When I See A Rainbow (406.)
235. An Angel Gives Me The Finger (407.)
    Forget Death (I'm Not Scared) **(913.)**

(Side Four)
236. Living Life On The Moon (541.)
237. Hello, Welcome to Planet Earth (569.)
238. I Say This To You World (480.)
239. Standing In Blood Stains (Holding A Flower) (542.)
240. My After Death Life (597.)

(Bonus Songs)
Pain And Laughter (526.)
Gemini Mind (607.)

221. The Pig People Are Back

I-Want-This and That
Got to Show-Off
My-New-Thing – I-Just-Bought
Don't-Matter if I – Can-Afford-It or Not
Look-Around – How-Can- I-Not
When everybody Else has it Already

I-Can't-Seem – Like a Without
To-All the People-That
I-Don't-Want to Know
And-Don't-Want to Know-Me

(Chorus)
The Pig People Are Back
Worshiping Greed And Lust
Slaughter And Mayhem
The Pig People Are Back
Wanting To Own The World
And Wallow In Its Muck
Come On Pig People
Do Your Oink-Oink Dance

Sex is For-Sale – Everywhere
When the Lustful – Want to Play
They-Pull-Up – To a Corner
Look at The-Merchandise – Then-Pick
The-One-That-They're – Willing to Pay-For

It's an Easy-Thing – You-Can-Have-It
Real-Fast or You-Can-Have-It – Real-Slow
If-You-Pick the Wrong-One
You-Can-Even – Wind-Up-Dead

(Repeat Chorus)

Government's-Become too Thick
The-Man-Never – Gets-Tired
Of-Stepping-On-Us – So-They-Can
Keep-Climbing – Higher and Higher
Keeping-Us – Out of Sight
For-They-Don't – Want to Look at Us

They-Know – They-Don't-Have-To
For-We-Are-All – Just-Pigs to Them
That-Might-Need to Be-Slaughtered
If-We-Ever – Want to Know-For-Sure
What's-Really – Going-On-With-Them

(Chorus)
The Pig People Are Back
Worshiping Greed And Lust
Slaughter And Mayhem
The Pig People Are Back
Wanting To Own The World
And Wallow In Its Muck
Come On Pig People
Do Your Oink-Oink Dance

222. Make Love Not War

Out of Nothingness – Came-Life
One-Moment – There-Was-Our
Non-Living – Planet-Earth
Just-Spinning-Away – All-Lonely
Looking-For a Passing-Stranger
To-Make-Her – Come to Life

Lucky for Us – Came a Big
Chunk-Of a Past-Living-Planet
Passing by With-Nothing to Do
He-Said – Bang-It – Think-I'll
Pass-Along – My-Seed

(Chorus #1)
Make Love Not War
It's Really Freaking Easy
You Hate Filled – War Mongering
Pieces Of No Peace In You
Pieces Of Loveless Crap

(Chorus #2)
Make Love Not War – Or Go War
Some Where Else – Because
Mother Earth Is Sick Of It
And Just About Ready – To Kick
The War Out – Of All Of You

One-Day – There-We-Were
Top of The-Food-Chain
Destroying and Killing-Everything
Like-Nothing is Sacred – Any-More
Not-Caring – About-The-Price
That-Our-Not-Caring is Costing-Us

When-Mother-Earth – Says
If-You-Want-War – You've-Got-It
As-She-Takes-Away – All-Our-Air
Then-Freezes – Herself-Frozen
Ridding-Herself – Of a Human-Plague

(Chorus #1)
Make Love Not War
It's Really Freaking Easy
You Hate Filled – War Mongering
Pieces Of No Peace In You
Pieces Of Loveless Crap

(Chorus #2)
Make Love Not War – Or Go War
Some Where Else – Because
Mother Earth Is Sick Of It
And Just About Ready – To Kick
The War Out – Of All Of You

223. My Wish Is

Came to The-War by Plane
Flying in With – My-Fellow-Warriors
Feeling-Their – Inner-Strength
Gives-Me a Feeling of Inner-Power
The-Thing-We-Need to Survive

Knowing-We – Can-Count-On
One-Another to Get – The-Job-Done
So-More of Us – Will-Make-It – Out-Alive
So-It-Will-Take – Less of Us
Warriors to Win-This-War

War-Never-Stops – Its-Endless
Bloody-Battles – Every-Day
Makes-You-Hard – Makes-You-Smart
Ready and Able to Take-Out
The-Enemy as They-Appear

(Chorus)
My Wish Is – To Serve
My Country – The Best I Can
Make It Out Of This War Alive
So I Can Go Back Home
Living The American Dream

My-Times-Almost-Up – Few-Days
I'm-Going-Home – Broken
The-War is Still – Going on Strong
Too-Many-Warriors – Still-Dying

War is a Body-Hungry – Creature
That-Never-Stops-Eating – It-Just-Keeps-On
Chewing and Swallowing – Both-Sides-Up
I-Can't-Wait to Get as Far-Away
From-War as I-Can

(Chorus)
My Wish Is – To Serve
My Country – The Best I Can
Make It Out Of This War Alive
So I Can Go Back Home
Living The American Dream

224. What's Next

Catch a Cold – Die a Week-Later
Mankind – At a Loss
What to Do – What to Do
Is-This-Natural – Is-This Man-Made
Mother-Earth – Science
Which-One – Will-Kill-Us-First

(Chorus)
What The Hell Happened
Is God Pissed Off At The World
Did Mankind Do It Again
Is The Devil Happy as Hell
That We're Dying Very Fast
All I Can Ask Is – What's Next

Jam-That-Needle in Deep
Feel-That-Rush of Healing
The-Cure – The-Forever-Cure
Finally – We're – Saved
Half-The-World is Dead
Other-Half – Needs-The-Cure

(Chorus)
What The Hell Happened
Is God Pissed Off At The World
Did Mankind Do It Again
Is The Devil Happy as Hell
That We're Dying Very Fast
All I Can Ask Is – What's Next

Caught-Off-Guard – We-Believed
Hard-Drug – Better-Than-Death
Now-We-Are – Not-The-Same
World is Full of Addicts
That-Don't-Want -to- Save-The-World
Just-Ready to Keep-On – Jamming and
Jamming-The-Cure – Into-Their-Veins

(Repeat Chorus)

(Save The World: In Two Parts)

225. I. Wood And Metal Eaters

Beautiful and Sunny-Day
We-Try to Forget-The-Pain
From a World – That's-Gone-Insane
It's-The-Way of The-World
With-Humans – Killing-Humans
Because – Humans-Hate-Humans

Humanity – The-Dominate
Humanity – The-Top of The-Food-Chain
Humanity – Thinks-They're-Safe
Now-It's too Late – We're-Doomed

(Chorus)
Wood And Metal Eaters
Eat Up All The Pretty Flowers
Wood And Metal Eaters
Eat Up All The Pretty Trees
Wood And Metal Eaters
Eat Up All The Tall Buildings
Wood And Metal Eaters
Eat Up All The Long Bridges

One-Day – Everything is Fine
The-Next-Day – Humanity-Watches
As-Small-Machines – From-Space
Swoop-Down and Start-Eating-The-World

Fight-Fight – Save-The-World
Wood-And-Metal-Eaters
Can be Destroyed – They-Can-Die

(Chorus)
Wood And Metal Eaters
Eat Up All The Pretty Flowers
Wood And Metal Eaters
Eat Up All The Pretty Trees
Wood And Metal Eaters
Eat Up All The Tall Buildings
Wood And Metal Eaters
Eat Up All The Long Bridges

II. Flesh And Bone Eaters

Mankind – The-Proud
Mankind – The-Disturbed
Both-Their-Bloods – Seed-The-World
Grab-Your – Man-Made-Ray-Gun
Shoot and Destroy – All-The-World-Eaters

They-Can-Not be Reasoned-With
They're-Machines – With-Teeth
Alone be Eaten – Together be Saved
Grab-Your – Man-Made-Ray-Gun
Shoot and Destroy – All-The-World-Eaters

(Chorus)
Flesh And Bone Eaters
Eat Up All The Pretty Women
Flesh And Bone Eaters
Eat Up All The Handsome Men
Flesh And Bone Eaters
Eat Up All The Pretty Girls
Flesh And Bone Eaters
Eat Up All The Handsome Boys

Grab-Your-Sick – Grab-Your-Dying
Grab-The-Criminals – Grab-The-Insane
We-Need a Blockade – This is Our-Chance
Fun-For-All – We-Live – They-Die

Saving-The-World – Is a Big-Responsibility
Drink-Your-Beer – Kiss-Your-Lover
Grab-Your – Man-Made-Ray-Gun
Shoot and Destroy – All-The-World-Eaters
Fight-Fight – Save-The-World

(Chorus)
Flesh And Bone Eaters
Eat Up All The Pretty Women
Flesh And Bone Eaters
Eat Up All The Handsome Men
Flesh And Bone Eaters
Eat Up All The Pretty Girls
Flesh And Bone Eaters
Eat Up All The Handsome Boys

41

226. Kick You In The Mind

Times-Have-Changed
The-Angry – Have-Won
Forgetting – What-They
Fought-For – For so Long

Laughter is Dead
Pain and Self-Pity
Is-What-Makes – This-World
Spin and Get-Turned-On

(Chorus)
Kick You In Your Mind
Kick You In Your Ass
It's The Same Thing
You Bunch Of Ass Minds

Being-Who – You-Want to Be
Was-The-Freedom
Worth-Fighting-For
The-More – The-Mightier
With-Voices so Strong

Became-The-Unheard
While-The-Pushed-Overs
Time to Finally-Shine
Came on Strong
Then-Became – Total-Hate
For-All – That-Use to Be

(Chorus)
Kick You In Your Mind
Kick You In Your Ass
It's The Same Thing
You Bunch Of Ass Minds

There-Was a Lot of Bad
No-Freaking-Doubt
But-There-Was a Lot of Good
War and Hate – Should-Breed-Love
If-Not – What's-The-Point

Life is For-Everything
Take a Break – From-Your-Hate
Have-Some-Fun – Maybe-Get-Laid
Buy a Pizza – Have a Drink
Get-Laid – Get-Laid – Get-Laid

(Chorus)
Kick You In Your Mind
Kick You In Your Ass
It's The Same Thing
You Bunch Of Ass Minds

227. Prick of Flesh

Bullets and Brandy
Sidewalk – Sandwiches
You're in Fear – Every-Day
Hate is All – You-See

Love is Dead and Gone
Fear-Has – Risen-Bright
Lonely-You-Look – Into-The-Mirror
The-Wall-Behind-You – Is so Dirty

(Chorus)
Prick Of Flesh
Fear In Your Eyes
You're Slipping So Fast
Snap Out Of It You Damn Fool
Before You Take Your Own Life

Take-Your-Time – Think it Over
Tomorrow is Another-Day
Hell-Will – Be-In-It
Don't-Pray-For-It – To-Go-Away

Make a Slice of Happiness
It's-Not-Easy – With-Will of Mind
A-Mountain – Can-Be a Stone
A-Drop of Water – Can-Be an Ocean

(Chorus)
Prick Of Flesh
Fear In Your Eyes
You're Slipping So Fast
Snap Out Of It You Damn Fool
Before You Take Your Own Life

Rain-Today – Rain-Tomorrow
Cabin-Fever – Growing-Doom
Your-Flesh is Crawling
Walk-Out that Door and Face-It

No-Pureness – No-Release
It's-Just-Rain – That-You-Feel
A-Gift of Life is Lost
Lightning-Strikes – Beside-You
The-Jolt of Almost-Death
Awakens-Your – Want-For-Life

(Chorus)
Prick Of Flesh
Fear In Your Eyes
You're Slipping So Fast
Snap Out Of It You Damn Fool
Before You Take Your Own Life

Thick-Darkness – Turns to Gray
Your-World is Changing
Love-Might be Behind-The-Door
That-You're – Staring-At – So-Nervously

What-Will – You-Do
You-Packed – Your-Bags
They're in Your-Hands
You're-Frozen at Your-Door
With-Your-Mind – Starting to
Question – The-Sanity of It-All

(Chorus)
Prick Of Flesh
Fear In Your Eyes
You're Slipping So Fast
Snap Out Of It You Damn Fool
Before You Take Your Own Life
44

228. The Blue Planet Red And Dead

Burning-Hell – With-Fury
Fiery – Leather – Wings
Warrior-From-Hell – Is-Coming
Gonna-Rip – His-Way-Up
From-Far – Down-Under

(Chorus)
Satan Is Waiting
For Mankind To Die Out
He Gets To Own All The Souls
That God Doesn't Want
He Also Gets To Turn
The Blue Planet Red And Dead

Being-The-First to Burn
Making so Many-Suffer
Loving it Lots – Getting-Turned-On
Satan-Wants to Party on Earth
Enjoying – Burning-Evil – Sex-Everywhere

(Chorus)
Satan Is Waiting
For Mankind To Die Out
He Gets To Own All The Souls
That God Doesn't Want
He Also Gets To Turn
The Blue Planet Red And Dead

Hell-Has-Been – Taken-Over
The-Warrior of Hell
Decided to Kill – Satan-Instead
The-Big-Party is Coming-Home
Freedom – No-More-Pain in Hell
Just-Lots of Drinking and Getting-Laid

(Chorus)
Satan Is Waiting
For Mankind To Die Out
He Gets To Own All The Souls
That God Doesn't Want
He Also Gets To Turn
The Blue Planet Red And Dead

229. It Was Just Yesterday

We've-Been-Together
For-Five-Years-Now
Both of Us so Much
Still-In-Love
With-The-Other

Some-Would-Say
That-We – Have-Been
Living-In-Sin
For-The-Past – Few-Years

Hell-With-Them
We-Love – Each-Other
It-Is-Our-Love
We-Make – Great-Together

(Chorus)
It Was Just Yesterday
We Were In Love
Gonna Get Married
Oh Why To Hell
Did That Mad Monster
Have To Come Around The Corner
And Shoot You In Your Head

Everything-Was – Going so Fine
Hard-Times-Always – But the Love
We-Shared-Together
Kept-Us-Strong and Honest

You-Never – Went-Out-Looking
Neither – Did-I
Some-Might – Call-Us-Boring
We-Would-Just-Laugh
Kissing – Each-Other-Madly

(Chorus)
It Was Just Yesterday
We Were In Love
Gonna Get Married
Oh Why To Hell
Did That Mad Monster
Have To Come Around The Corner
And Shoot You In Your Head

We-Were-Suppose to Be
Two in Love – Forever
Going to Help – The-Other-Out
After-We-Both – Grew-Up

Having-Our-Normal
Day-In and Day-Out-Lives
Happily-Living-Them – Together
Making a House – For-Our-Future-Family

I-Am so Sorry – That-It-Was-You
Instead of Me – That-Got-Shot
You-Would-Have –Made-Such a
Wonderful-Mother – Our-Love
Together – Would-Have-Been-Enough

To-Teach-Our-Children
Right-From-Wrong – so
They-Would-Not – Grow-Up
Becoming a Evil-Monster
That-Shoots-Someone – Like-You
In-Their-Alive – Only-Once-Head

(Chorus)
It Was Just Yesterday
We Were In Love
Gonna Get Married
Oh Why To Hell
Did That Mad Monster
Have To Come Around The Corner
And Shoot You In Your Head

Life Is Too Short

Life-Is-Too-Short
Death-Comes – Too-Soon
Are-You-Happy – Are-You-Sad
Does-Your-Mind – Fear-Life
Does-Your-Mind – Fear-Death
You're-Not-Alone – You're-The-Same

Mother-Earth is For-Everyone
While-You're – All-Alone
Searching-For-Love
While-Never-Leaving – Your-Home

(Chorus)
Life Is Soft – Life Is Hard
Tomorrow Might Not Be Your Day
Take Your Dream – Change It
Into Something That Changes Your Life
Because – Life Is Too Short
To Watch The World Pass You By

One is The-Loneliest – Number
Maybe it's True – Maybe it's Not
I-Have a Wife – That-Loves-Me
Do-I-Love-Myself – I-Feel-Like-I-Do
Even-Though – I'm-Scarred

Can't-Blame – The-World
For-Being so Fickle and Grand
Can-I-Blame – The-World
For-My-Dreams – Not-Coming-True
Will-I-Die-Tomorrow – or
Will-Tomorrow – Be-My-Day
Only-One-Way to Find-Out

(Chorus)
Life Is Soft – Life Is Hard
Tomorrow Might Not Be Your Day
Take Your Dream – Change It
Into Something That Changes Your Life
Because – Life Is Too Short
To Watch The World Pass You By

230. My Force

I-Need- Money – Man-Do-I-Need-It
I-Know – What-You're-Thinking
Who-The-Hell – Are-You
What-About-Me – I-Need-Money-Too

Well-You're-Right of Course
But-What – Can-I-Do
Gotta-Think of Myself-First
World-Has-Taught – Me-This

I'm-Not-The-Same – You-Think
I've-Turned-Ugly – I-Gotta-Make-It
Life is For-The-Doers – Not for The-Kick-Backers

(Chorus)
Moving Way Too Fast
To Slow Down Now
Step Aside Or My Force
Will Knock You Down
As I Go Passing You By

I-Know-I've-Changed – I-Don't-Care
Love-Me or Hate-Me – I'm-Not-Stopping
Just so I – Can be Like-You-Again

I-Live-Alone – With-My-Success
My-Life-Consists of Darkness
I'm so Lonely – Being-Alone

Got-My-Huge-Victory – But-I-Don't-Have-Anyone
To-Share it With – If-I-Could-Go-Back – I'd-Do
The-Same-Thing – This-Time-I-Would Take the Time
To-Stop-Awhile – For-Some-Sun – Fun and Love

(Chorus)
Moving Way Too Fast
To Slow Down Now
Step Aside Or My Force
Will Knock You Down
As I Go Passing You By

231. Time Is In My Eyes / Weak God People

Time Is In My Eyes

Time-Is-In-My-Eyes
I-Don't – Sing a Sad-Song
I'm a Happy – Forevermore
That's-Been-Here – Since-Day-One
Because-You – Hate so Much

Time-Is-In-My-Eyes
Watch to See if I-Blink – Can't-Help
To-Laugh – You-Bunch of Praying
Fools – That-Needs a God so Much

(Chorus)
Time Is In My Eyes
Will I Be Here Tomorrow
Was I Here Yesterday
You Don't Understand – And
You – Never – Will
(Repeat)

Weak God People

Don't-Care a Flying-Freak
I'm the One that's Going to Survive
Day by Freaking-Day – Let-The
World-Bleed – I-Will-Not

Sin-Me – Sin-You – I-Laugh
That-Crap – Doesn't-Effect-Me
Don't-Care a Flying-Freak
If-I'm – Without a Soul

(Chorus)
Bring It On – Weak God People
Eat Your Sins Up – With Your Asses
As I Walk Proudly Away From You
For I Don't Want You – And
I Don't Need Any Of You
Weak God People
(Repeat)
50

232. Freedom With Sex

Smash-That – Glass-Ceiling
Don't-You – Feel-Your-Pain
How-Much – Will-You-Take
'Til-You-Realize – The-Crap
You-Have to Deal-With
Should be Outside – Your-World

(Chorus)
Freedom With Sex
Is Pure Freedom Of Choice
Don't Bring Hateful Sex
Bring Freedom Sex
It's So Much Purer – And
It Don't Fill You Up With Hate

Smash-That – Glass-Ceiling
He-Likes-Her – She-Likes-Him
He-Likes-Him – She-Likes-Her
No-One-Gets – What-They-Want
While-You – Have to Fear-Your-Choice
For-What – Might-Happen to You

(Chorus)
Freedom With Sex
Is Pure Freedom Of Choice
Don't Bring Hateful Sex
Bring Freedom Sex
It's So Much Purer – And
It Don't Fill You Up With Hate

Smash-That – Glass-Ceiling
Is it Right – Is it Wrong
Maybe to You – Maybe to Them
I-Don't-Care – What's-The-Difference
You-Have-Yours – Let-Them-Have-Theirs
Don't-Matter as Long as Both of Them – Say-Yes

(Repeat Chorus)

233. Tag, Tag (Tag You're It)

You-Walk-Free and Alone
Looking for Something-New
Something-That – Makes a Difference
In-Your-Cold and Lonely-World

You've-Been-Hurt – You've-Been-Betrayed
Saying-Never-Again – Will-You be Fooled
By a Stranger's – Cleaver-Hateful-Words
You-Know-Now – Wrong-From-Right

(Chorus)
Tag, Tag – Tag You're It
Here – Take My Holy Pain
Here – Take My Greedy Hate
Tag, Tag – Tag You're It
Help Me To Own The World
Help Me To Destroy The World
Tag, Tag – Tag You're It
What Do You Say – Will You Help Me Today

Time is Ticking in Your-Head
Your-Need is Not-Being-Fed
Why-Does a World – With-Everything
Have-Nothing – That-Turns-You-On

You-Say-No but You-Stop-Anyway
Listening to The-Power of God
From a Man That-Speaks – Hell's-Fire
Damnation is Still – Coming to End
And-Still-You – Haven't-Changed

(Chorus)
Tag, Tag – Tag You're It
Here – Take My Holy Pain
Here – Take My Greedy Hate
Tag, Tag – Tag You're It
Help Me To Own The World
Help Me To Destroy The World
Tag, Tag – Tag You're It
What Do You Say – Will You Help Me Today

234. When I See A Rainbow

I-Don't-Know – I-Feel
Like-I'm – Slowing-Down
Life-Doesn't – Taste the Same
Brightness is Dulling
Getting so Hard on Me
To-Want to Even-Listen

The-Ringing of My-Phone
Makes-Me – Want to Flee
Always-Somebody on The-Line
Wanting to Talk-About-Pain
And-Death – I'm so Frustrated
I-Feel-Like-Talking – About-Life

(Chorus)
When I See A Rainbow
It's Always In Black And White
Never Am I Allowed
To See And Feel The Colors
That Everybody Else
Takes For Granted

I-Need a Life-Injection
Something-Fresh and New
Helping-Me-Get – Out of This-Funk
I'm-Not-Having a Good-Time – Living-With

Walking-Down – My-Hall
Looking at My-Memories
Picture of Me in My-Youth
Falls to The-Floor – Crashing
Right in Front of My-Eyes

(Chorus)
When I See A Rainbow
It's Always In Black And White
Never Am I Allowed
To See And Feel The Colors
That Everybody Else
Takes For Granted

Taking-Out – My-Photo
From-All – The-Broken-Glass
Staring at It – I-Notice
It's-The-Brightest-Thing
I've-Seen – In-Years
With-Amazement – I-Smile
As-My-Life – Starts to Come
Back-Fully – Alive-Once-Again

(Chorus)
When I See A Rainbow
It's Always In Black And White
Never Am I Allowed
To See And Feel The Colors
That Everybody Else
Takes For Granted

235. An Angel Gives Me The Finger

Being a Pissed-Off – A-Hole
Is a Very-Easy – Way to Live
Never do You – Have to Worry
About-Another and Their-Feelings

This-May – Not be The-Best
Way to Get – Ahead in Life
A-Lot of Times – You-Never
Have to Worry – About-Friends – or
Getting a Second-Date

(Chorus)
I Try To Repent
For The Life I Lived
I Did My Best To Keep On
Living The Right Way
But When I Finally Reach
The Gates Of Heaven
An Angel Gives Me The Finger

Looked-Around – One-Day
At-Myself and My-Life
I-Didn't-Like – What-I-Saw
So-I-Packed-Up – All-My-Crap
And-Took – The-Hell-Off
Trying to Find – My-Heavenly-Way

My-Road to Salvation
Was a Very – Bumpy-One
Finding – The-Lust of Sin
Is-Always so Easy to Find
So-I Kept – My-Pants-On
With-My-Eyes – Half-Shut

(Chorus)
I Try To Repent
For The Life I Lived
I Did My Best To Keep On
Living The Right Way
But When I Finally Reach
The Gates Of Heaven
An Angel Gives Me The Finger

After-Years of Saying – No to Myself
I-Feel-Good – About-My-Life – and
My-Chance at Getting – Into-Heaven
I-Stayed – My-Same-Boring-Self
As-I-Aged to My-Death-Day

The-Pain is Intense as I-Die
I-Feel – Solid-Inside
I-Know – I'm a Lucky-One
As-I-Close – My-Eyes and Slip-Away
As-My-Soul – Flies-Towards-Heaven

(Chorus)
I Try To Repent
For The Life I Lived
I Did My Best To Keep On
Living The Right Way
But When I Finally Reach
The Gates Of Heaven
An Angel Gives Me The Finger

Forget Death (I'm Not Scared)

Am-I-Smiling – What-Kinda
Stain – Is on That-Wall
Never-Mind – It's-Not-Blood
Why-Would it Be

She-Said – She'd-Call-Today
Alone-I-Wait – Am-I a Fool
Can't-Blame-Her – I-Have a Problem

Damn-Death – Coming-After-Me
Nobody-Believes-Me – Not-Even-Her
Let-Me-Sing – My-Rhyme

(Chorus)
Forget Death – I'm Not Scared
Forget Death – I Can Only Die Once
Forget Death – I'm Tired Of Its Crap
Forget Death – Forget Dying
Hey-God – Hey-Satan – Let's Talk
About Me – Living-Forever And Λ Day

Death-Showed-Up – Last-Night
While-I-Was – Taking a Break
While-I-Was – Making-Love

She-Freaked – Now – She-Believes-Me
While-Death – Stood-There
In-Waiting – Silent and Still
For-Me to Be – All-Alone

Silly-Me – I'm-Safe – She's-Not
She's-Next –On-Its-List
Let-Me-Sing – My-Rhyme

(Chorus)
Forget Death – I'm Not Scared
Forget Death – I Can Only Die Once
Forget Death – I'm Tired Of Its Crap
Forget Death – Forget Dying
Hey-God – Hey-Satan – Let's Talk
About Me – Living-Forever And A Day

56

236. Living Life On The Moon

Looking-Down – From-The-Moon
Blue-Planet – Shines so Bright
I-Miss-Earth so Much
Exiled-From it Forever
Because-They-Say – I'm a Criminal

I-Tried to Spread-Freedom
In a World – That-Wanted
Nothing – But to Be-Controlled
Everyday is The-Same
Human-Life – Keeps-On
Even-Those – Who-Are-Cast-Out
Make-Their-Mark – With-Spirit

(Chorus)
Living Life On The Moon
Makes You Dead Inside
No Air – No Sun – No Love
Only Cold Fast Death
If You Can't Take It Any More

The-Man is Everywhere on Earth
Freedom is Dying so Fast
As the Moon-Becomes – Over-Populated
By-Those-That – Don't-Belong-Anymore

We're-Coming – Back-Home
Mother-Earth – Please-Welcome-Us
Love and Freedom is Alive-Again
The-Oppressed – Made-The-Difference

The-Man-Believed – They-Were-Gods
Only to Come to The-Cold – Hard-Reality
When-They-Were – Voted-Out
By-The-Too-Tired of Them-All

(Chorus)
Living Life On The Moon
Makes You Dead Inside
No Air – No Sun – No Love
Only Cold Fast Death
If You Can't Take It Any More

57

237. Hello, Welcome to Planet Earth

Saints and Sinners
Porno-Stars and Killers
Smiling-Faces – With-No-Teeth
Gray-Skies and Brown-Grass
Damn-World – You-Look so Fine

Junkies – Jabbing-Their-Arms
Babies – Thrown-In-The-Trash
Religious-Nuts – Burning-Books
Governments – Living-It-Up-Fat
Damn-World – You-Look so Fine

(Pre-Chorus)
Dying – Blood On The Ground
Death – Fumes In The Air
Pain And Lust Living Together
Like They Are The Same Thing

(Chorus)
Hello, Welcome To Planet Earth
Where No One Has Freedom
Hello, Welcome To Planet Earth
Where Hate – Sex And Death Rule
Hello, Welcome To Planet Earth
How Many Days – Would You Like To Stay

Is-What-I-Say – Too-Ugly
Well – No-Freaking-Crap
What-Can-We – Do-About-It
I'm-Only – Two-Things – And
Damn-World – You-Look so Fine

You-Don't-Need – We's-Help
We're-Way too Different for You
It's-Okay – We-Understand
It's-Not – Your-Fault – And
Damn-World – You-Look so Fine

(Pre-Chorus)
Dying – Blood On The Ground
Death – Fumes In The Air
Pain And Lust Living Together
Like They Are The Same Thing

(Chorus)
Hello, Welcome To Planet Earth
Where No One Has Freedom
Hello, Welcome To Planet Earth
Where Hate – Sex And Death Rule
Hello, Welcome To Planet Earth
How Many Days – Would You Like To Stay

We-Have-No – God or Devil
We-Do-Love – Life a Lot
We-Don't-Like to Kill or Destroy
But-We-Do-Like to Make-Love
Damn-World – You-Look so Fine

Hello-World – We-Can-Make a Difference
If-You-Let – We-Stand-Beside-You
Together as One – We-Will be Able
To-Make-That-Difference – For
I-Am-Peace and Harmony
The-Reaper of Evil and Injustice
Damn-World – You-Look so Fine

(Pre-Chorus)
Dying – Blood On The Ground
Death – Fumes In The Air
Pain And Lust Living Together
Like They Are The Same Thing

(Chorus)
Hello, Welcome To Planet Earth
Where No One Has Freedom
Hello, Welcome To Planet Earth
Where Hate – Sex And Death Rule
Hello, Welcome To Planet Earth
How Many Days – Would You Like To Stay

238. I Say This To You World

Why-Do so Many of Us
Have to Die – Unnecessarily
Why-Can't – Mankind-Stop
Killing – One-Another

When-Will – There-Be
Love of One-Another
When-Will – All-The-Children
Be-Completely-Safe

I-Don't-Know – Children
Are-Children to Me – Not
What a Monster – Wants-Them to Be
Love and Sex – Are-That to Me
I-Love – Them-Both
I-Want-It – In-Return
Never by Forcing – Someone

(Chorus)
I Say This To You World
You Freaking Suck
You Suck So Much
And You Don't Even Know It
But I And We Do Now

I-Know – Who-I-Am
Still – I-Don't-Know
What-I'm – Suppose to Be
Can't-Seem to Find-Out
From-Anybody-Else – Not-Even-We

The-Blood of The-Good
Keeps-Getting-Spilled
By-The-Bad and Hateful
Should-I – Close-My-Eyes to This
Just-Like – Everyone-Else

Tickles-From-Insanity
Comes-Around – For-Relief
I-Always – Laugh-Them-Away
Knowing-I'm – In-Control – of
More-Than-One – In-My-Mind

(Chorus)
I Say This To You World
You Freaking Suck
You Suck So Much
And You Don't Even Know It
But I And We Do Now

After-Contemplation – I-Bring
My-Mind – Out to Play – To-See
If-It-Can – Make a Difference
It-Tries – Very-Hard – Then
Quickly-Becomes – Cracked – And
Starts to Fade-Away – So-I
Quickly-Grab – It-Back-Up
For-Some – Mental-Healing

It-Takes – Some-Time
For-My – Fragile-Mind
To-Become – Crystal-Clear
It-Thinks-Out – Once-Again
I-Give-It a Flick – Asking
What's-Wrong – With-You
Saying – You're-Just a Mind
And-You – Don't-Matter

Then-Suddenly – Like a Sad
Crapped on Rainbow – Crawling
It-Came-Back to Me – Fully
Now-That-I – Have-Full-Control
I'm-Going to Use-It – For-Myself

(Chorus)
I Say This To You World
You Freaking Suck
You Suck So Much
And You Don't Even Know It
But I And We Do Now

239. Standing In Blood Stains (Holding A Flower)

Hello-Sick-Hating-World – We-Know-You-Hate-Us
You-Tried to Change-Us – But-We-Wouldn't-Let-You
Our-Changes – Come-From-Within
Stay-Out of Our-Heads – Let-Us-Be

You-Won't-Do-That and We're-Tired
Of-Asking if Death is Beautiful
When-You-Hate-Everything – Mother-Earth
Cries-Unheard by Her-Hating-Children

(Chorus)
Standing In Blood Stains
Holding A Flower
Looking At A Rainbow
Is The Way We Will
Change The World
Come Join We – If You Care

Death on The-Streets – Death at Home
Mr. Death is Way – Too-Busy
As-Blood – Flows-Free
Like a River – Across-The-World

We-Show-Up – With-Thick-Skins
Looking at The-Carnage
We-Know-Better – Than-To
Try to Spread-Love

Humanity is Not-Ready
They-Have-Not – Killed-Enough
Hopefully – One-Day-Soon
All-The-Blood-Flow – Will-Start to Look
Bad – Ugly and Not-Needed

(Chorus)
Standing In Blood Stains
Holding A Flower
Looking At A Rainbow
Is The Way We Will
Change The World
Come Join We – If You Care

240. My After Death Life

Way-Off in The-Distance
Is-Where-My – Dead-Body-Lies
All-Very – Bloody-Torn – From-War
In-My-Soul – I-Ponder
Walking to Find – My-Body

Is-There a Heaven – That is Lovely
Is-There a Hell – That is Brutal
Souls-Everywhere – Walking on Bodies
This-Bloody-Battlefield so Many-Died
Only-Blessing-Is – No-More-War

(Chorus)
All By Myself After Death
My Soul Is Strong
Still I Hunger For Life
My After Death Life
Is Only Temporarily Mine
As I Pray To God To Save Me

Fire is Rising – From-Out of The-Ground
Making the Battlefield's – Blood-Boil
The-Ground-Shakes – With a Hell-Bang
Satan is Not-Smiling – Standing-There
As-He-Burns – Souls to Dust

Shaking-From-Fear – Walking-No-More
I-Run-Like-Hell – Away-From-Satan
Hand-From-The-Sky – Reaching-Down
Picking-Up-The-Souls – That-Are-Not-Burning
Giant-Hand-Above-Me – Will-I be Picked-Up

(Chorus)
All By Myself After Death
My Soul Is Strong
Still I Hunger For Life
My After Death Life
Is Only Temporarily Mine
As I Pray To God To Save Me

Pain and Laughter (526.)

Born-Like a Rock – Cast-Out to Sea
No-Family – No-Home – No-Love
My-Life-Is a Living-Hell – Full of Fun
Drifting for Years – Taken-In by Strangers
Fed and Used – Tomorrow's-Just
Another-Day – For-The-World to Use-Me

(Chorus)
I Like My Hell
It's Easy To Understand
Everyday Is Full Of
Pain And Laughter
That I'm Allowed To Live
With Complete Content

Being a Nobody is Smart
I-Look-The-Same as Everybody
Nobody-Knows – My-Name
Or the Size of My-Being
I-Get to Walk-Away
Unseen and Unnoticed
As-Death – Stays-Behind-Me
I'm-Not-Cursed – The-World-Is

(Chorus)
I Like My Hell
It's Easy To Understand
Everyday Is Full Of
Pain And Laughter
That I'm Allowed To Live
With Complete Content

Living-My-Dream – Living-My-Nightmare
Reality-Is so Mind-Numbing – Unreal
I-Let-Fantastic – Fantasy
Live-Inside-Me – As a Comfort-Pad
For-The-Too-Much – That is Too-Real to Believe

(Repeat Chorus)

(Bonus Song)

Gemini Mind (607.)

In-My-Mind – I'm-Not-Alone
Being a Gemini – Since-Birth
Becoming-More – Two of The-Same
Becoming-More – Two of The-Different
As-I-Drifted – Alone in Life

Learning to Cope – With-Two
Voices-Talking – Inside-My-Mind
Trying to Make – Me-Become
Sane/Insane at The-Same-Time

(Chorus)
Mind Oh Mind
What Are You Going To Be Thinking
When You Enlighten And Rip Apart
My Being – As You Create Everything
With Your Gemini Mind

Along-With-Beauty and Peace
There's-Also-Pain and Death
Skipping and Stomping
Through-My-Mind
As-We-Do – Their-Best and Worst
Keeping-The-Earth's – Conscious and
Unconscious – Flowing-Free and Torn

(Chorus)
Mind Oh Mind
What Are You Going To Be Thinking
When You Enlighten And Rip Apart
My Being – As You Create Everything
With Your Gemini Mind

Happiness and Rainbows – Sadness and Bloodstains
Building and Destruction – Beginning and The-End
I-Have a Gemini-Mind – That-Keeps-This-World-Alive
Love and Hate – Peace and Death – I'm-The-Gemini-One
Come-Mind-Rockin' – Mind-Dancing – With-We

(Repeat Chorus)
65

The Chemical Lightning Man (The Lyrical Story)
(Songs 711-720) (Pages 66-77)

Chapter One:
No Pain – No Fear (711.)
Take My Time (So I Don't Break You) (712.)

Chapter Two:
Found Him – Laid Her (713.)
I Am Chemical Lightning Man (714.)
Payback Is A Bitch (715.)

Chapter Three:
Paint The World Red (716.)
From Wanted Criminal To Hero Trilogy: (717.)
I. Blood On My Hands
II. No More Blood
III. I Am A Powerhouse

Chapter Four:
Pig Mosh Of Blood And Flesh (718.)
You Die Now (I'll Die Later) (719.)
World (Alone I Stand Tall) (720.)

No Pain – No Fear (711.)

I-Was – No-One-Special
I-Was – No-One to Remember
Then-One-Night – What-I-Saw
Was to Become-The Death of Myself

Injected-With-Toxins
I-Was-Dying so Very-Bad
Lightning – Struck-Me
Once – Then-Twice – I-Was
Reborn – Something-Different

(Chorus)
Pain – I Feel No Pain
Fear – I Have No Fear
Stay Out Of My Way
Or Be A Fool And Die
Pain – I Feel No Pain
Fear – I Have No Fear
Go Ahead – Point Your Gun At Me
Go Ahead – Shoot Yourself

From-Out of An-Outer-Shell
I-Breathed a New-Life
Day by Day – I-Searched
The-Streets for Scum
That is Willing to Take
Their-Very-Own – Lives by
Their-Very-Own – Hands

Every-Day – I-Live-Another-Day
Every-Day-Scum – Dies-The-Same-Way

(Chorus)
Pain – I Feel No Pain
Fear – I Have No Fear
Stay Out Of My Way
Or Be A Fool And Die
Pain – I Feel No Pain
Fear – I Have No Fear
Go Ahead – Point Your Gun At Me
Go Ahead – Shoot Yourself

Take My Time (So I Don't Break You) (712.)

Come on Baby – Here-I-Am
A-Very-Different – Kinda-Man
That-Just-Saved – Your-Life
They-Would-Have – Killed-You

You-Would be Dead – Right-Now
If-Not for My – Bullet-Proof-Body
So at The-Least – Baby
You-Should – Make-Me-Smile

(Chorus)
Don't Worry Baby
I'll Take My Time
So I Don't Break You
Enjoy Me Baby
As I Take My Time
Changing You For Life

What's-Wrong – Pretty-Baby
You-Need to Take a Break
I-Understand – I-Understand
Tell-You-What – Baby
Why-Don't-You – Call a Friend

Have-Her – Come-Over
She-Can – Take-Your-Place
Just-Make-Sure – She is Fine
Because – Pretty-Baby
I-Don't – Lust-With-Skanks

(Chorus)
Don't Worry Baby
I'll Take My Time
So I Don't Break You
Enjoy Me Baby
As I Take My Time
Changing You For Life

Found Him – Laid Her (713.)

My-Creator – Is a Pig
Sick-Rich – Get-In-My-Way
Everyone-That is Not-Him
You-End-Up – Dead
The-World is His-Feeding-Stock
The-World is His-Personal-Toilet

(Chorus)
I Have Questions
My Creator Has Answers
The Pig Was Still Dealing In Filth
When I Found Him
So I Made Him Watch Me
With His Secretary – As I Laid Her

She-Loves-Me – He-Hates-Me
She-Wanted to Stay – With-Me-Forever
He-Wanted to Crawl-Away – Wishing-Me-Dead

Play-Time is Over – Chemical-Pig-Man
You-Made-Me – What-I-Am – I-Hate-You
Then-Again – Maybe-I-Should – Thank-You
That-All-Depends on Your-Answers
Whether-You-Live or Whether-You-Die

(Chorus)
I Have Questions
My Creator Has Answers
The Pig Was Still Dealing In Filth
When I Found Him
So I Made Him Watch Me
With His Secretary – As I Laid Her

I Am Chemical Lightning Man (714.)

I'm-Cursed – I'm-Blessed
I am More – Than a Man
I am More – Than-Human
I'm a Mistake – Gone-Wild

Mess-With-Me – You'll-Fry-From-My
Chemical – Lightning – Strikes
Mess-With-Me – While-Getting-Laid
I'll-Melt-You to Ash – With-My-Chemical
Mist-Spray – Then go Back to Getting-Laid

(Chorus)
I Am Chemical Lightning Man
Come Take Your Weak Shot
I Am Chemical Lightning Man
You Can Beg Or You Can Die
I Am Chemical Lightning Man
I'll Melt You To A Chemical Mist
I Am Chemical Lightning Man
I Am Forever – I Will Never Die

Powers – My-Powers-Are-Many
Bullet-Proof – Long and Hard
Chemical – Lightning – Strikes
I'm-The-Answer to Your-Pain
Pleading – Will-Not-Help-You

Armies-That-Attack-Me – Will-Fail
Push-Me-Too-Far – You'll-Learn
That-Your-Fear and Hate
Will-Only-Bring-You – Your-Death
While-I-Walk-Away to Get-Laid

(Chorus)
I Am Chemical Lightning Man
Come Take Your Weak Shot
I Am Chemical Lightning Man
You Can Beg Or You Can Die
I Am Chemical Lightning Man
I'll Melt You To A Chemical Mist
I Am Chemical Lightning Man
I Am Forever – I Will Never Die

Payback Is A Bitch (715.)

You-Have so Much-Money
Chemically – Swimming-In-It
Owning-Your-Big – Piece of The-World
Like-You – Deserve-It

Test-Subject – You-Wanted-Me-Dead
All in The-Name of Capitalism
Life of Mine – Meaning-Nothing
To a Chemical-Pig – Like-You

(Chorus)
Pay Back Is A Bitch – Creator
You Wanted Me Dead – I Feel
The Same Way – Only You Instead
Pay Back Is A Bitch – I'll Return
Your Favor – Bring You – Your Death
Pay Back Is A Bitch – And You Deserve It

You-Made-Me a Mistake
I'll-Make-You a Mistake
I-Live – You-Die – Damn-Fool
Should-Have-Helped – Feed-The-Poor

World is Beautiful – I'm a Monster
I-Just-Wanted to Live-My-Life – Now
I'm-Chemical – Lightning-Man
Now-You-Are a Dead – Creator
Time for Me to Get-Laid – After
I-Drink a Lot of Alcohol

(Chorus)
Pay Back Is A Bitch – Creator
You Wanted Me Dead – I Feel
The Same Way – Only You Instead
Pay Back Is A Bitch – I'll Return
Your Favor – Bring You – Your Death
Pay Back Is A Bitch – And You Deserve It

Paint The World Red (716.)

Evil and Sick is Everywhere
The-World – Loves to Kill
Blood-Here – Blood-There
Have to Watch – Where-I-Step

My-Mind is Clicking
Blood-Here – Blood-There
Will-The-World – Ever-Get-Enough
I-Don't – Think-So

(Chorus)
It's Not My Fault
The World Loves Blood
I Just Want To Get Laid
It's Not My Fault
That I Can Not Take Any More
It's Not My Fault – That I Want To
Paint The World Red
Paint The World Red

People-Love-Me – People-Hate-Me
I'm a Chemical
Lightning-Monster on The-Loose
Am-I-Right – Am-I-Wrong
I-Don't-Know – Anymore

The-World is Still-Filled – With-Bad
As-I-Wipe-My-Eyes – Clear of Blood
Blood-That's-Infected – My-Mind
There's-Got to Be a Better-Way

(Chorus)
It's Not My Fault
The World Loves Blood
I Just Want To Get Laid
It's Not My Fault
That I Can Not Take Any More
It's Not My Fault – That I Want To
Paint The World Red
Paint The World Red

(From Wanted Criminal To Hero: Trilogy) (717.)

I. Blood On My Hands

Life-Is a Bitch – That-I-Live
Realizing-Blood – Is on My-Hands
Nobody's-Like-Me – I'm-All-Alone
Species of One on This-Planet

Mind's on Fire – Pounding-Like
Thunder in The-Night-Sky
I-Did-Not-Want – This-Power
I-Did-Not-Want – My-Hands
Stained – Red

(Chorus)
Blood On My Hands
Rocket In My Pocket
Am I Good – Am I Bad
It's So Hard To Tell
With All This Thick
Blood On My Hands

II. No More Blood

I'm-Down – In a Hole of Despair
How-Do-I – Climb-Back-Out
When-Part of Me – Feels-No-Remorse

There-Has to Be a Higher
Reason – For-My-Existence
Got to Focus – Got to Save the Good
From-All-The-Bad – In-The-World

I-Have-The-Power – I'm-The
Chemical – Lightning – Man
When-The-Bad – Try to Kill-Me
They-Get-Their – Own-Blood
On-Their-Hands – Not-Mine

(Chorus)
No More Blood
On My Mighty Hands
No More Blood
Will I Be Bleeding Out
No More Blood
I Will Help The World

III. I Am A Powerhouse

I've-Become – Mr. USA
Blood-Stains – My-Hands
Every-Bloody – Single-Day
All-The-Evil of The-World
Stop-Killing – Keep-Yourselves-Clean
Or – I'll-Step on Your-Souls
Don't-Blame-Me – Blame-Yourself

(Chorus)
I Am A Powerhouse
That Feels No Pain
For Making The World Bleed
I Am A Powerhouse
That Is Backed By The USA
I Am A Powerhouse
That Controls The World

I've-Become – Mr. USA
Blood-Stains – My-Hands
Every-Bloody – Single-Day
All-The-Evil of The-World
Stop-Killing – Keep-Yourselves-Clean
Or – I'll-Step on Your-Souls
Don't-Blame-Me – Blame-Yourself

(Chorus)
I Am A Powerhouse
That Feels No Pain
For Making The World Bleed
I Am A Powerhouse
That Is Backed By The USA
I Am A Powerhouse
That Controls The World

Pig Mosh Of Blood And Flesh (718.)

I-Was-Rich – I-Had-Power
Used-Everything – Used-Everybody
For-My – Greediness of Life
Blood and Lives – Meant-Nothing
For-Me – All-For-Me

Piece of Crap – Who-I-Destroyed
Came-Back-Into-My-Life – Like a Plague
Changing-Who-I-Am – Leaving-Me for Dead
As-I-Became – The-Chemical-Pig-Man

(Chorus)
Pig Mosh Of Blood And Flesh
I Eat Humans Every Day
Still I'm So Hungry – For More Meat
Pig Mosh Of Blood And Flesh
I Come To Your Town
And Eat Everyone Around
That Tastes Deliciously Sweet

Stomach so Large – Always-Empty
I-Eat – All-The-Weak – Humans-Up
They-Scream and They-Scream
While-I-Eat-Them – Alive to Death

Skin so Thick – I-Feel-No-Pain
Tanks-Planes – I-Melt to Nothingness
With-My-Pig-Ass – Mist of Burning-Death

I'm-The-Top of The-Food-Chain
Even-Chemical – Lightning-Man
Fell to The-Ground – Like-Weak-Prey

(Chorus)
Pig Mosh Of Blood And Flesh
I Eat Humans Every Day
Still I'm So Hungry – For More Meat
Pig Mosh Of Blood And Flesh
I Come To Your Town
And Eat Everyone Around
That Tastes Deliciously Sweet

75

You Die Now (I'll Die Later) (719.)

Evil-May-Never-Die
But-Monsters-Do
Hit by Hit – He-Squealed
Chemical – Pig – Man
Trying-His-Best to Hit-Me-Back
Finding-Nothing – In-Return but Air

(Chorus)
You Die Now – I'll Die Later
I'm The Hero – You're The Monster
You Die Now – I'll Die Later
You've Eaten Your Last Human
You Die Now – I'll Die Later
Burn In Hell – Chemical Pig Man

Stomp – Stomp – Stomp
I-Keep-Him-Down – In-Pain
I'm-The-Hero – I-Cannot-Die
Out of Nowhere – Pig-Ass-Mist
In-My-Eyes – Up-My-Nose
I'm-Going to Die – Soon

(Chorus)
You Die Now – I'll Die Later
I'm The Hero – You're The Monster
You Die Now – I'll Die Later
You've Eaten Your Last Human
You Die Now – I'll Die Later
Burn In Hell – Chemical Pig Man

Rage in My-Soul – Pole in His-Heart
Chemical-Pig-Man – Dies
Shitting-Out – His-Pig-Shit

Walking-Away – Not-Wanting to Die
Life is Most-Definitely a Bitch
At-Least-The-Pig – Died-First

(Repeat Chorus)

World (Alone I Stand Tall) (720.)

World-You – Fucking-Suck
I-Destroyed – I-Killed for You
I-Almost-Died for You
What do I – Get in Return

All-You-Want is More
Like-The-Pig – People-You-Are
Now-It's-Your – Time to Give
Complain – All-You-Want
I-Don't-Give a Shit

(Chorus)
World – Alone I Stand Tall
This You'll Never Understand
World – Alone I Stand Tall
I Don't Need You – You Need Me
World – Alone I Stand Tall
Love Me – I'm Forever – You're Not

Time-Brings-Me – What-I-Want
Gold – Women and Beer
The-Chemical – Lightning-Monster
Loves to Bring-Down – The-Pain

Mankind – Plead-All-You-Want
You-Had-Your-Chance at Peace
Now-It's-Out of Your-Hands
Right-Into-My – Blood-Soaked-Ones

Don't-Piss-Me-Off – Maybe-I'll
Chill a Little-Bit – Don't-Count on It
Unless-World – You-Prove-Yourself-Worthy
Of-My-Returning to The-Chemical-Lighting-Man

(Chorus)
World – Alone I Stand Tall
This You'll Never Understand
World – Alone I Stand Tall
I Don't Need You – You Need Me
World – Alone I Stand Tall
Love Me – I'm Forever – You're Not

The Chemical Lightning Man (The Story)
(Pages 78-91)

Chapter One:
Rebirth Of Someone Different
Sex, Have To Be Careful,They Break So Easy

Chapter Two:
Find My Creator
I'm A Mistake
You're A Mistake

Chapter Three:
Chemical Lightning Monster On The Loose
Regret / Cleanse Myself Clean / Mr. USA

Chapter Four:
Chemical Pig Man Returns
Fight To The Death
A Hero's Death

Chapter One:
Rebirth Of Someone Different

"Can I do anything for you Chemical Lightning Man?"

"No, I'm dying just fine however you can sit with me as I die and listen to my story of how I became a hero, my biggest mistake. My story starts over twenty years ago, I was working at a chemical company when I walked in seeing what they did not want me to see. They freaked, as I appeared standing there watching them load toxic crap in containers marked nontoxic onto a truck in the dark. They gathered around me, I prepared to fight for my life. Things calmed down when Mr. Big Toxic Dumping himself offered me a lot of money to keep my mouth shut.

I am no fool. I said yes right away without thinking about it, letting them know I was greedy and wanting out of this alive. My payday was the next day, which was fine with me because as soon as I was free I was going to take a quick trip to my pad then I was going to get as far away as possible from the shit I stepped in. They let me go, watched me leave my place, then they snagged me, tied, gagged and blindfolded me. The ride I was given lasted about an hour or so. I was thrown out of their van like a piece of trash while listening to them tell me how short my life was."

"Lightning ripped across the sky and thunder roared like a big bass drum as storm clouds came rolling in, then the rain came pouring down. It came down so hard and fast that I could not hear their endless banter anymore. Then out of nowhere I was injected with a needle, then a second, then a third. I shook as different kinds of pain gave me their worst. My heart was pounding so fast, so hard, it felt like it was going to pound out of my chest. My skin at first felt like it was becoming thin taffy, only to change to become hard as rock and roll. Same with my bones, at first they felt like they were turning to dust, then with very hard and painful snaps they reformed thicker, harder than rock and roll."

"I was walking, well stumbling around as my steps became harder for me to take. I felt myself becoming harder and heavier with each painful step. The noise of the storm stopped just like that, moments later lightning struck me, I paused still standing, feeling a little better.

I was starting to get a little happy about the idea of playing dead when once again I was struck by lightning, this time the strike not only knocked me off my feet but it knocked me out. When I woke up I thought I was in a coffin. Man was I wrong. What was going on was, I was inside an outer shell that I had to break myself free from."

"This took forever, I almost gave up. My first attempts at breaking free from my shell had no effect at all. Then little by little, like an egg shell, it started to crack. The more of my outer shell that gave way the more momentum I had, the stronger I felt. When I was finally free, standing naked looking at a clear night sky, well things went very unexpectedly for me. I thought about going to a hospital or to the police but after fully checking myself out I more than knew there was no need for me to at all. Just like now, I was thick all over and hung which made me so happy. What I had before never made any ladies complain, the new me however, well I became every woman's fantasy or nightmare come true. While I walked away I stepped on some of my outer busted up shell, it crunched underneath my feet and caused no pain or cuts."

"Curiously, I picked up a piece of my outer shell and walked over to a tree to see how sharp it was. With this small piece I could cut chunks out of the tree without any of it breaking off. I then took the piece of shell and tried to cut my arm, nothing, not even a mark. Moments later I was doing some more experiments on myself, like punching that same tree, it shook from my force and my hand was fine, better than ever. I was naked, laughing at the night, watching my outer shell dissolve when somebody bad decided to come up to me and try to rob and kill me. Bad man said, 'Where's your clothes you naked freak? Better yet where is your money?' I said nothing, wondering to myself if I was bullet proof?

Bad man got mad and told me that he was going to kill me. Bad man pulled the trigger of his gun as I lifted up my right hand, palm up to him, the bullet bounced off my hand and struck him right between the eyes and dead he fell to the ground. The first of many fools who killed themselves by trying to shoot me. I picked up his gun, I felt this burning fire inside myself, out of my mouth came this burning green chemical mist that melted the gun to ash in my hand. I took his clothes that barely fit me and his money of course and got the Hell out of there. On my way to anywhere, a pimp came up to me and asked me if I wanted to be with one of his ladies. I told him I didn't Fuck skanks, dumb pimp pulled out his gun and fired it at me.

80

I walked away with all of his and his ladies' money, while he laid there dead with a bullet from his own gun stuck in his head."

"In a week's time I had over one hundred thousand dollars inside my very expensive pants that fit my metal, rock hard body like a glove. Every night after that for awhile I did the same thing, making more money as more dumb asses killed themselves with their own guns, sometimes more than one at a time. I felt like a God inside an indestructible, sexy body."

Sex, Have To Be Careful, They Break So Easy

"Before I get to the first bloody meaty part, let me tell you this stranger. I read a lot of superhero crap and there's this time frame sometimes. I had no idea how long the new me would stay like that. And if I did loose my powers, would I revert back to who and how I was before or would I die from not having powers anymore, making my body so weak that it disintegrated just like my outer shell did?

I admit it, I was freaked out for awhile, so I didn't get laid for those first few weeks. The first time was so out of sight. This fine little lady was being assaulted so I walked over to help her. The two monsters who thought they could do anything that they wanted to her, for they were strong and she was weak, did not like this very much. First monster pulled out a knife, I laughed and told him that I would stick his knife in the top of his head. Second monster laughed with me then said, 'So you're not afraid of knives? Let's see if you are afraid of guns? Let's see if you are bullet proof?' I still laughed as I told monster number two, "Yes I am, bullet proof that is."

"Once again without even one touch from my hands, bad people were dead and I was taking their money. Out of the corner of my eye, I spotted the little sexy lady walking over to me, scared and turned on. She looked at me like I was from outer space, then she asked me if I was going to hurt her. I told her no. She thanked me, then asked me if there was anything she could do for me as a thank you very much. I told her what I would like as my thank you very much. She straightened out her dress, grabbed me by my hand, she kissed me, then told me to come with her to her apartment that was only one block away. She was a very experienced at giving a man some pre-loving before sex kinda lady, if you know what I saying?

Well to make a large subject turn small, at the end of our loving encounter, she kinda got broken a little bit. My fault, for I had no idea what the intensity of getting to the point where I smile was doing to her body and more importantly her love slice. I felt so bad after having the greatest explosion I have ever felt, looking at her crying and still wanting more of what I had. So I gave her a hand full of money and dropped her off at a hospital. I am proud to say with that some trial and error, I have become one great man for a lady to meet if she is looking to have an encounter that will change her for life."

"Hang on stranger, while I pause to remember one more time a lady that I will never forget. What I would not give to enjoy her one more time, in that sexy looking time of her life because by now she probably has a fat ass."

Chapter Two:
Find My Creator

"Stranger are you ready for some bloody meaty part?"

"Yes I am, Chemical Lightning Man. By the way my name is Ted Hazeltrip, I am a reporter. I am recording your story, your death for a book that I am writing about of your life as a hero, your great deeds, your love life and your sins. You were like a blessing to the world, other times we felt you came from Hell like a nightmare that we could not wake up from."

"I am so proud of you for putting all those words in a row like that, Ted Hazel-Ass-Trip-Face, now if you are ready to shut the Fuck up, I'll continue my story!"

"Sorry Mister Chemical Lightning Man, please continue."

"I had money, I had thankful women so I felt it was the time to find the people that had done this to me, a bunch of payback and total erasing of what happened to me, to prevent it from being used against them. Makes a lot of sense doesn't it Ted?"

"Yes Mister Chemical Lightning Man."

"Mister? I like that show of respect Ted. Who knows, I've had so many women, young man, I could be your Daddy, Ha, ha, ha."

"No Sir, my Father was..."

"Shut your ass Ted. I'm dying here. If you piss me off, who knows, I might just melt you to ash, just to add one more fool to my list of thousands of fools."

"I wanted answers, so I staked out the chemical plant from a car I had borrowed. Finally with four ass kissers in line and one hot Secretary, here came Mr. Did This To Me. I followed them to a meeting. When they got back in their limo I was driving it. I took them into the bowels of New York City. Mr. Did This To Me was not very cooperative at first, so I made two ash piles with two of his ass kissers, then I broke his left hand and he talked. Man did he talk, so much so that I had to slow him down just to keep up with him. I stopped him before he got

too far because I wanted to make this ordeal for my Creator last as long as possible and I wanted to have some fun at his expense. I had his hot Secretary tie the two remaining ass kissers up and told her to kick them, she kicked them a few times then asked me if it was alright if she just hit them with her shoe instead. I told her yes and watched her beat the shit out of these two ass kissers so much that she made them both cry.

My Creator watched in horror as his hot Secretary asked if it was time for her to beat my Creator now. I laughed and told her to come to me. We kissed while I squeezed down on my Creator's broken hand. A few minutes later myself and hot Secretary were naked, she paused and walked over to my tied up Creator and shoved her panties deep into his pleading for help mouth."

"We had our fun for an hour or so, hot Secretary fell in love within the first five minutes. I used her love for me to have her get into my Creator's bank account. She was so grateful and in love with me she even set up an account for me so I could own all his money. I was so pleased with her work, I gave her some of my Creator's money and one more time of what she really wanted so very badly. When we finished I did not kiss her goodbye, she left walking away with what to do next in her life going through her, wanting to do this all over again tomorrow, mind. So happy, so sad just like life truly is."

I'm A Mistake

"Reporter Ted, you look turned on."

"That was a hot tale Chemical Lightning Man."

"That Ted was just a small scratch to how much sweet tail I've enjoyed from there to here. Always remember I am not a comic book hero. I have blood on my hands. But mostly people, scumbags in general, took their own lives when they tried to shoot me. Ted even though I am almost invincible when someone tried to stab or beat me with something, I felt that they deserved the same back to them with what they tried to use against me. And yes Ted, everyday I got laid.

I am horny all the time, the chemicals that were injected in me not only made me so much more than I could dream of being, but also gave me a very big Thunder-Stick that is ready to go all the time. Even more my Thunder-Stick is a hot woman's best friend that she has not met yet and after she does, she wants to be friends with my Thunder-Stick for the rest of her life. That Ted is Fucking Beautiful , I am so proud of myself for batting over a thousand."

"I don't know what to say. I could never imagine having that much sex."

"Of course not Ted, you're just a man, a little one at that, ten percent of the amount of sex I had would wear you down to a happy fast death. You don't have what I have and you don't have it inside you to do with it what I can without even trying. Don't feel bad Ted, no man on this planet can keep up with my Thunder-Stick, while most women cry from the might of it. Alright enough of my Thunder-Stick. Ted, you want to know more about my creation don't you?"

"Yes I do Chemical Lightning Man."

"I'll continue on then Ted."

"I was a mistake my creator made, I was only to become dead from different ways from the effects of different chemicals and serums. My creator begged for his life as I told him to shut up and tell me more of what happened to me after the second lightning strike that struck me and the outer shell that I broke myself free from.

There were five men who took me for my ride, only one of them made it back to my creator to tell him of what happened due to the two lightning strikes that was not in the plan of my controlled death. Ted say this word with me. 'Absorbed'. That's right Ted, 'Absorbed'. The second lightning strike struck me down and unconscious, the five men watched me as I laid there apparently dead. A green substance expelled from my body, fast enough to snag four out of the five men. They screamed as I 'Absorbed' their beings to become my outer shell. My creator, #5 and others came to visit me, they tried like heck to break my shell made from man to get to me. What happened was, that's right, I 'Absorbed' up some more bad men making my human shell even thicker, with the addition of more human clay to make my shell even more grand."

You're A Mistake

"I have a saying Ted. Pain for pain, blood for blood, payback is a bitch. My creator was so sorry, wanted to be my benefactor. Told me he would do anything he could, anything I needed or wanted to make my creation more enjoyable. I had already made two ash piles that blew away in the bowels of New York, so I figured two more would not make much of a difference. That being done I grabbed up my creator threw him in his limo and drove us back to his chemical plant. When we got there I made him show me what was injected into my body and all the video footage of me and my shell.

I read all the information on what was injected into me. Some very scary and dangerous stuff was injected into me Ted. I could not believe after reading what I read that I was still alive, let alone become what I am today. It was the lightning Ted. When I was struck, somehow the chemicals painfully flowing inside me changed my body chemistry to something that has never been before. This bothered me and also excited me at the same time."

"I was a mistake that was very pissed off, looking for payback that was considered a bitch for my creator. So I slapped my creator around some, making him bleed out like the chemical pig that he was. That being done, I took what was injected into me and some more nasty chemicals and injected them into my creator, making him a mistake this time. I laughed my ass off Ted, watching my creator move around in a tremendous amount of pain just like I went through weeks ago.

85

My creator was taking his last steps when I grabbed him, walked him over to some electrical equipment, pulled out some live wires and then Ted, I shocked the shit out of him. He jumped around like his insides were on fire. I laughed and told him to suffer like the piece of shit, chemical pig that he is.

Ted, with no remorse I watched my creator take his last few painful breaths, then with one great last desperate gasp he departed on the floor. I was just about to walk away leaving him like that Ted, but something inside my mind told me that I was not quite done yet. So with great feeling going through my mind I burned that sick ass chemical plant down to the ground."

"I went home, washed all the nasty off my body, got dressed and headed to a bar which I almost drank dry. Then in the early morning light I took three women with me back to my home and enjoyed all three of them at the same time until all four of us passed out from four or five hours of great group sex."

Chapter Three:
Chemical Lightning Monster On The Loose

"Ted, I think I'm dying now?"

"Don't die yet you haven't finished your story."

"Ted you are a pig of a reporter. Lucky for you I'm fucking with you. I just wanted to know what was more important to you, my life or my story. I have enough life left in me Ted, to go on, to lead to this moment that we are sharing together. You want more blood Ted?

Welcome to the part of my story, my darkest moments where I was not considered a man but a monster that needed to be stopped. Ted at this point in my life, I just got my payback, very bloodily at that. I did not know what to do with myself, I was always horny and ready to go, yet out of nowhere bad men kept coming up to me wanting my money and my life. After so many times there is no way in my mind that it was random acts of violence anymore, for Ted, around every corner there was someone waiting for my chemical scent to seep into their senses and invade their minds to make the violence level inside them increase ten fold or more.

There is a great thing about this Ted, only men get the killing urge from me. Women, Ted that's another story, women get turned on from my chemical scent. I've watched as women walked away from their men and right up to me for me to reset their clocks. At first it was what it was. I was going on just fine, then time took its toll on me Ted. I walked up on women getting attacked for more than just their money. Even sadder Ted I walked up on children being used in sick ways. The world became a world full of hate and shit to me. Ted, mercy no longer had a meaning to my mind and being."

"Something clicked inside me Ted. I still took the bad man's money but it was their blood on my hands that I was more interested in. So every night I went out looking for as much blood as I could find to soak my hands in. The police came out in droves to stop me. Did them no good. Finally, after awhile they stepped out of the way to let the military have its chance of taking me out. I never had to fight back just protect myself. I was half mad but coherent enough to know that it was not their fault but mine, that they had to do whatever it took to stop me from killing anymore bad men. I was all over the news of the world, I was labeled a Chemical Lightning Monster on the loose and the world was afraid that after I got done with all the bad men, I would come after them. So sad this hit me. I took a break and explored my mind for some contemplation of inner peace."

Regret / Cleanse Myself Clean / Mr. USA

"Ted I got to take a piss. So while I crawl to that wall to take a piss in this beautiful alley of New York City, I want you to get me a beer or six."

"Right away Chemical Lightning Man."

"Ted, I don't know why but when you say my name it makes my ass have a painful itch. Don't say anything I'm in pain. Go get my beers while I piss blood out with my piss."

Ted walks away and as soon as he is out of sight 'C.L.M.' stands up tall almost healed from his wounds fully erect and ready for some sex action but first he has to pull off his plan that makes him dead and not fucked with anymore by the world's many problems. When Ted gets back with a six-pack 'C.L.M.' is laying back down in pain wanting a beer to drink.

"That's better. Damn good beer Ted, give me another one. As you can tell Ted I was in a fucked up part of my life, I was so down, so I decided to give myself up and after many conversations the great United States of America decided that I was too important to lock up for my crimes. Instead Ted I became the one that was put up front and center for all other countries to see so very well, as an understanding, 'If you fuck with the USA you fuck with me', and I will come to your country and kick your ass all in the name of the USA and freedom."

"I regret much about what I did Ted, however saving the USA everyday made me feel like I cleansed myself clean from all the pain that I was feeling. I knew better, I knew I was being used but people loved me and gave me lots of money. And the women, Ted they stood in line just to get to wait longer after finally getting their number. I still got blood on my hands but now it was sanctioned blood, which made all the difference to me as a blessing to be as mighty as I needed to be when the world stepped out of line and started up some blood slaughter. They all thought they were so strong and mighty, then I would show up and just fuck them all up, wipe my ass on their faces, use their women, and take their gold as payment for making me kick their asses."

"Life was going so great Ted, I was Mr. USA, I had anything I wanted given to me on a silver platter by women dressed in hardly anything. Then one day, Hell, a cold hard reality came into my life changing everything. I'll get to that part as soon as I drink down a couple more of these wanted and needed beers."

Chapter Four:
Chemical Pig Man Returns

"Ted sometimes the things a person does out of not caring or out of malice comes back to you like a kick to your insides. Should have, could have just flooding your mind from your mistakes. Life has a balance. I am a single, no one was my opposite. This earth could not make one for me. Out of pissed-off-ness and the certain right going through my mind, when I decided the fate of his ending, well Ted I fucked up bad, I made something that makes me look like a bad school boy just being bad. The Chemical Pig Man returned from the brink of death to cause slaughter by the bloody buckets of it. I could not believe what I created Ted. I created something that not only killed people but ate them up like a top predator.

I'd show up where he was eating and he'd be gone, leaving blood and bones all over the place. Before long Ted, the Chemical Pig Man had eaten ten thousand people all over the world. Even worse, all this heavy on me turned me off, it took so much just for me to finish my sexual moments that I knew something had to be done with the Chemical Pig Man. I thought long and hard, I even went without getting any tail for a couple of days. So Ted, you know I was serious at the moment when I decided I needed to roast this human eating, Chemical Pig Man to charred burning flesh."

"Reality Ted has a way of resembling fantasy, when like a comic book I fought the bad guy and lost. Bad guy left me laying on the ground all bloody and fucked up, laughing as he walked away like a dumb ass, giving me my opportunity at a second chance to bring him down. Unlike a comic book where the hero risks their lives just to bring the bad guy to justice for their crimes, this was not my way of handling the final battle. Justice had to be served but a death was called for even more."

"Lessons learned from our first battle Ted, were very much on my mind as I healed from my scars and bruises. My creator that I created as well was one strong and powerful, nasty ass smelling monster who smelled like he was dipped in shit. My bad guy was so inhuman that even during our battle he stopped to eat someone new more than once. My hits, my punches, my kicks felt like I was hitting something that had so much thick skin on its hide that the pain from them did not register until later. When he was walking away I noticed that he was starting to lean and drag from the pain given to him, coming back to him all at once. Stamina had to be my concern as I made myself stronger, strong enough to win by ripping him apart slowly and surely."

Fight To The Death

"Ted I'm out of beer and I need to take another piss. Go forth young man, bring me my ale for I am almost to the end of my story and I feel my death coming to me faster than before." Same scene as before, 'C.L.M.' cleared his head some more, ready to make himself dead to the world as Ted went to buy some more beer. 'C.L.M.'. drinks three beers silently before he restarts his story. "Ted, it is time for the end of my story. 'C.P.M.' had no worries, no fears, only thing on his mind was who to eat next. Sickly sometimes he started to think with his small head as he gathered pretty women together for his own harem.

Ted, can you imagine being one of these pretty woman, so use to having sex with good looking men and now to sink so low as to have this ugly 'C.P.M.' all over your fine body? Life is most definitely not fair Ted."

"'C.P.M.' was eating on somebody's legs when I caught up to him, he smelled me coming from miles away. With no fear of me in his mind he just kept eating like I had no matter to him at all. So Ted I walked up to him and kicked him up his ass, point of boot right to his A'hole. I laughed my ass off watching him get so mad trying to kick me back. He tried so hard to kick me Ted, that he even fell on his ass from missing me so hard. When he fell to the ground I stomped on him and stomped on him, laughing as he told me was going to eat me. Finally he got up and I just kept hitting him then backing out of the way so his strikes back to me hit nothing but air.

Eventually Ted 'C.P.M.' became so tired he fell down exhausted, then I stomped on him some more. I felt invincible as 'C.P.M.' grew weaker, I was in Heaven as he started to bleed, first just a little then the pig was bleeding buckets of blood."

"I left him lying there as I walked over to a street sign. I ripped of the stop symbol ready to use the pole as a spear to kill 'C.P.M.'. Ted he was belly up squealing like the pig he is when I brought down my killing strike. 'C.P.M.' caught me off guard as he sprayed me with his chemical pig-ass mist, right into my face, blinding me as I breathed it into my lungs. My eyes cleared as the burning grew more intense inside my body. I knew it was too late for me I was already dying. 'C.P.M.' was getting to his feet as I struck him with everything I had, sending the stop sign pole straight through his heart. 'C.P.M.' stood there for a moment with the pole through his chest, then he fell down leaking out his piss and shit on the ground as he died. I walked away from his shitty smell to this alley, where I plan to die, meeting you."

A Hero's Death

Ted watches in silence as a hero's death comes closer to the Chemical Lightning Man. Ted watches as shaky hands try to open the last beer of twelve. Ted is a prick that can't wait to see the Chemical Lightning Man die, not out of some dark meaning but for the greatness his death will bring to the end of his book.

90

Ted is now thinking how great he is, starting to pay less attention to the actual death and more to the dramatic one that will be his grand written version. "Here Ted have the last drink of the last beer that I will ever drink. I feel pretty good for dying Ted, there is hardly any pain, I'm at peace. Don't want to die but alas I am and I will not go out crying about my life begging God to let me into his Heaven. No Ted I'm going out all hard and ready as a rock, man that I am."

"That is the perfect way for you to die Mr. Chemical Lightning Man, you saved the day, you saved the world, now die like the bad ass that you are. But before you die I want you to know that I will make you sound as much as a monster as the Chemical Pig Man. As far as I am concerned both of you were the biggest mistake ever to be brought to life on Earth. I am glad that he is dead and will be even more glad after you are dead. I'm going to take off all your clothes, rub dirt on your face and ass then I'm going to take a lot of pictures of you looking like the piece of monster shit that you are. You deserve no better Chemical Lightning man, I just wish I could take away your powers before you die."

"Ted you prick, I'm not dying. I was going to fake my death and just live the rest of my life getting laid, saying fuck the World let it save itself from now on. But Ted since you are such a great person, typical of most people that live on this Earth, excluding most women of course, I've changed my mind." 'C.L.M.' gets on his feet and makes an ash pile out of Ted the Reporter and yells out to NYC, "fuck my Hero's Death, the only thing that died inside me tonight is my compassion, perhaps my humanity, shake with fear where you stand NYC and the rest of the World.

The Chemical Lightning Monster has been reborn and this time it is perhaps forever. You can hide your gold and your women but if they have any worth, I'll take them away from you and then it's up to you if you live or if you die. And one more thing fuck you for killing the Chemical Lightning Man inside me that wanted to save the world. My heart has only one more beat for this world, if you want it world you will have to do the changing this time, I've changed enough for you it is your time to do the changing."

YOUR OWN MIND ROCKIN' PAGE #2

Extra Stuff
The Extra Six
Fuck It, Here's Six More
(Pages 93-99)

(Side One)
If They Want To Hate (197.)
(Written: 9-??-2013)
(This Song Was Originally Book # 202.)

Survive This Night's Freeze (433.)
(Written: 01-08-2014)
(This Song Was Originally A Book 11 Bonus Song)

I Don't Want Any Candy Coating (527.)
(Written: 03-29-2014)
(This Song Was Originally A Book 11 Bonus Song)

(Side Two)
My Name Is Freedom (582.)
(Written: 05-24-2014)
(This Song Was Originally Book # 205.)

Kick That Dead Body (699.)
(Written: 01-28-2015)
(This Song Was Originally An Extra For Books 11/12)

Eat Crow A'Holes (748.)
(Written: 04-10-2015)
(This Song Was Originally An Extra For Books 11/12)

If They Want To Hate (197.)

Life is Good – Life is Bad
It's-Always – Hard on Us
We-Make-It – What-We-May
If-There-Is a Heaven or A-Hell
I-Don't-Want to Know
Anything – About-Their-Hate

All-I-know is What-My-Mind
Lets-In – I-Block a Lot-Out
Keeping-Myself – Safe-From-All
The-Hate-Shown to Me
No-Way – Will-I-Let-It
Corrupt-My – Peaceful-Mind

(Chorus)
If They Want To Hate
Let's Make Them All
Hate Themselves Even More
It's Our Right As Enlightened
To Have Peace And Love
In Our Lives Everyday

To-All-You-Haters
Preaching-Out – About-Your-Heavens
Why-Don't-You – Go to Your-Hells
That-You-Spent – Your-Lives-Creating
For-All of Us to Suffer-Through

Time and Time-Again
Getting-Into-Our-Lives – Endlessly
Keeping-Us-Stuck – In-The-Same-Place
Never-Being-Allowed to Get-Out-From
Under-All-Your-Constant – God-Funk

(Chorus)
If They Want To Hate
Let's Make Them All
Hate Themselves Even More
It's Our Right As Enlightened
To Have Peace And Love
In Our Lives Everyday

94

Survive This Night's Freeze (433.)

I'm-Very-Cold – Can-I-Get
Some-Warmth – I'm-Really
Really-Dirty – Hope-You-Can-Ignore
My-Scent of Trash and Filth

Even on This – Coldest of Days
Can't-Help-It – I-Try but I
Just-Can't-Seem – Able to
Wash-Away – The-Street
That-Covers-Me – In-Its-Nasty
Thick – Wet – Funk

(Chorus)
With A Little Bit Of Your Warmth
I Think I Might Be Able To
Survive This Night's Freeze
So I Can Die Another Night
Maybe Tomorrow – If I'm Unlucky

You-Feed-Me – I'll-Try-Not to Bark
I'm-Happy – That-I'm-Going to Survive
Being-Found-Dead – In-The-Streets
Is-In-The-Back of Everyone's-Mind
That is Just-Like-I – That
Live-Their-Lives – In-The-Streets

(Chorus)
With A Little Bit Of Your Warmth
I Think I Might Be Able To
Survive This Night's Freeze
So I Can Die Another Night
Maybe Tomorrow – If I'm Unlucky

Thank-You – For-This-Blanket
I'm-Going to Steal
I-Need-It – More-Than-You
Don't-Hate-Yourself – For-This
Feel-Glad – You-Gave-It to Me
Instead of Feeling-Like
You've-Been-Used and Betrayed

(Repeat Chorus)

I Don't Want Any Candy Coating (527.)

Up and Down – Nowhere in Between
The-Truth-Hurts – Too-Much to Tell
Lies-Are so Much-Prettier
When-Told so Proudly

Story-Doesn't-Matter
As-Long as We – Believe-In
What-They – Want-Us to Know
Watch as Only – Their-Guilty-Ones
Get-Punished – For-Doing-Nothing

(Chorus)
I Don't Want Any Candy Coating
I Like To Think For Myself
Instead Of Listening To Lies
That Speak To Me Ugly
As If They Were Truth
I Don't Want Any Candy Coating
Just Give Me The Truth

Right or Wrong
Is so No-Way – Anymore
To be Nice and Smiling
As-They – Tell-You-How it Is
Is-The-Key – For a Happy-Life

Believing-In – The-Same-Way
Making-Yourself-Ready
To be Copied – For-Exposure
Will-Only – Return-You to Clay
As-You-Unhappily – Live-Longer
Than-Those – That-Don't-Believe

(Chorus)
I Don't Want Any Candy Coating
I Like To Think For Myself
Instead Of Listening To Lies
That Speak To Me Ugly
As If They Were Truth
I Don't Want Any Candy Coating
Just Give Me The Truth

My Name Is Freedom (582.)

The-Stars – Have-Aligned
A-Power-Surge – Has-Risen
From-Deep-Down – Inside-Me
I-Hunger – For-Something
I-Have a Taste-For-It
But-I-Can't – Remember
What-I-Hunger – For so Much

I'm-Bleeding – I'm-Starving – I've-Been-Shot
I've-Been-Stabbed – I've-Not-Been-Fed

(Chorus)
I Waited – I Got Stronger
I Feel So Much Better
Now That I Remember
What I Am
My Name Is Freedom
This Time I Will Belong
To The Whole World
Not Just A Privileged Few

I'm-Angry – I'm-Sad – This-Sucks
Tired of The-Same – Damn-Thing
Everywhere is Death
Everywhere – There is Starvation
I'm-Tired of Being-Ignored
I'm-Freedom – Call-For-Me
Instead of Bleeding to Death

I'm-Bleeding – I'm Starving – I've-Been-Shot
I've-Been-Stabbed – I've-Not-Been-Fed

(Chorus)
I Waited – I Got Stronger
I Feel So Much Better
Now That I Remember
What I Am
My Name Is Freedom
This Time I Will Belong
To The Whole World
Not Just A Privileged Few

Kick That Dead Body (699.)

War-Time – Means-Dying-Time
Bodies-Here and Bodies-There
It's-Not-Even – Sad-Anymore
That-Time – Has-Passed-By – While-Sadness
Has-Been-Replaced – With-Fear

It's so Hard – Not to Laugh-Out-Loud
When-You-Have to Eat – Sleep and Crap
Next to Dead-Bodies – Left-Out to Rot
By-Those-Who – Love-War and Death

(Chorus)
Kick That Dead Body
Out Of Your Way
Kick That Dead Body
Make Sure You Keep Count
Kick That Dead Body
See If It Has Any Food
Kick That Dead Body
See If It Has Your Face

Peace to Me – Peace to You
Practice-What – You-Preach
Make-No – More-War

Forget – About-Heaven
Forget – About-Hell
Try to Live – Another-Day
Without-Letting – Killing
Be a Part of Your-Day

(Chorus)
Kick That Dead Body
Out Of Your Way
Kick That Dead Body
Make Sure You Keep Count
Kick That Dead Body
See If It Has Any Food
Kick That Dead Body
See If It Has Your Face

98

Eat Crow A'Holes (748.)

We-Are-Losers – You-Say
We-Do-Nothing – Your-Way
You-Like – Our-Votes
As-You-Take-Away – Our-Freedoms
We-Just – Don't-Understand

Your-Life-Is so Hard-On-You
And-It's-All – Our-Fault
That-We-Keep-Getting – In-Your-Way
Time-Heals – All-Wounds
Rebirth is Filled – With-Such-Pain
As-These-Words – Are-Sung to You

(Chorus)
Eat Crow A'Holes
You Deserve Everything You Get
Eat Crow A'Holes
Eat It Off The Ground
Eat Crow A'Holes
Choke It Down Your Holes

In-The-Distance – Freedom is Rising
You-Can-Quail-It – All-You-Want
Freedom – Will-Never-Die
Shame on Us – Shame on You
Hope-We-Can – Forget-This-Day
From-Ever-Happening – Once-Again

We-Are-Losers – You-Say
We-Do-Nothing – Your-Way
You-Like-Our-Votes – As-You-Take-Away
Our-Freedoms – Time-Heals-All-Wounds
Rebirth is Filled – With-Such-Pain
As-These-Words – Are-Sung to You

(Chorus)
Eat Crow A'Holes
You Deserve Everything You Get
Eat Crow A'Holes
Eat It Off The Ground
Eat Crow A'Holes
Choke It Down Your Holes

The Invention Of Mind Rockin'

I've always been a fan of music, classic rock, rock and roll, hard rock and heavy metal. I've also always been a fan of movies, comedy drama, action, suspense, fantasy and horror. As a kid my hobby was writing lyrics that I created in my mind. In 2013 I took my hobby, my passion for music and movies and with them I created Mind Rockin'. By doing so I made myself become something that I never thought or dreamed of doing before and that was to become a self-published author. My creation of Mind Rockin' works like this. I sit down in front of my computer and come up with a melody or score in my mind to go along with the original songs or lyrical stories that I am creating. However when you the reader/singer reads or sings the song or lyrical story, there is no right or wrong for the melody or score that you come up with in your minds, be it rock and roll, pop, country or rap. Mind Rockin' is a concept I created for persons just like myself, those of us that would like to be able to do or create something like stories or songs but with no opportunity knocking at the door this dream of ours stays that, a dream. Mind Rockin' is the only thing in the world where the person you are has the chance to use what's inside you instead of the usual way where it is only one way for everybody, and that is the way the creator intended for it to be foretold or heard.

I'd like to dedicate this book and thank my Wife of Twenty-Four years, I love you Christina thank you for your Love and Support.

I'd like to thank all my Family and all my Friends. Thank you to all my Fans, I am a Fan of yours as well, together We can make a difference. Let's Shout It Out and Speak As One.

The Gemini Rising Rockin' Machine.

"Who are you?"   "Who am I?"

"Yes, don't you know?"   "Not today, maybe not yesterday."

"You're dressed with the likes I've never seen."

"Yes I've noticed. Compared to what you're wearing, I must be so very strange looking, so very strange."

"Why do you have that breathing apparatus on your face? The air here is breathable. See, watch me breath in the air like it's almost pure."

"I don't know, I feel so strange, like I'm out of time."

"Well it's 11:38 am, the year in case you need to know is 2017."

"I do not know who I am but that's not possible. It is not 2017, it's 2037. I know this, I remember now. What a bummer."

"A bummer huh? Well man, when life brings you down, look into the sky at the sun and have a reminder that life is beautiful."

"Well man all I can say about that is that we have a lot of work to do."

"Look old dude, I'm trying to be cool and all but we have no work to do together."

"Well get this man, I am you, you are me. I am you from 2037, the year Mother Earth starts to die."

"Man you are tripping. I like to get high but damn man you are really stoned out of your mind if you truly believe it is 2037."

"Well dude hold on to your mind and balls, for the breathing apparatus is coming off."

Old dude takes off his breathing apparatus and the young dude freaks out. (I can't blame him this is pretty heavy.)

"Are you here to take me into the future?"

"No, me. I'm here to give you the heads up so you can start a revolution that will save Mother Earth from dying in 2037. Better get started you only have twenty years."

www.ingramcontent.com/pod-product-compliance
Lightning Source LLC
Chambersburg PA
CBHW071628140626

46555CB00021B/1246